RUNNING TOWARDS FREEDOM

A Young Adult Novel

L.F. Conrad

Copyright © 2023 L.F. Conrad

All rights reserved

The characters and events portrayed in this book are fictitious. Any similarity to real persons, living or dead, is coincidental and not intended by the author.

No part of this book may be reproduced, or stored in a retrieval system, or transmitted in any form or by any means, electronic, mechanical, photocopying, recording, or otherwise, without express written permission of the publisher.

ISBN-13: 9798387957048
ISBN-10: 1477123456

Cover design by: Art Painter
Library of Congress Control Number: 2018675309
Printed in the United States of America

*Dedicated to Bampy and Dubdub,
thanks for listening.*

CHAPTER 1

Molly Grace Ford stared at the ocean. She laughed as the dolphins jumped out of the crystal clear blue water. She watched as the waves rolled peacefully into the white sand. The sky was clear and blue, and Molly Grace had nothing to worry about. The green from the trees completed this extraordinary painted scene. If only Molly was there. In the beautiful state of Hawaii.

Molly Grace Ford resided in New York City in 1941. It was the chilly month of November. November 10 to be precise. She was an orphan, who lived at Miss D's Orphanage for Girls. As you can imagine, Molly did not have the most pleasant childhood. Her parents have been out of her life since she was very young. Ever since, she's been moving from orphanage to orphanage. Molly had stayed at this particular orphanage the longest though.

Molly had been at Miss D's since she was ten years old. Molly was now fourteen years old, almost fifteen. Molly's birthday was November 18. So Molly didn't have much longer until she was fifteen.

Molly Grace was a small girl. She had a small frame and was not tall whatsoever. She had long straight brown hair and her brown eyes were too big for her little face. Molly had a little smile and little nose. Even though her appearance on the outside was somewhat small, she was quite the firecracker. Being an orphan, Molly Grace had learned to stick up for herself.

Miss D's Orphanage for Girls was not in a good place in New York City. Some bad people hung around the streets and alleyways that surrounded the orphanage. Molly was one of the oldest girls there. So, Molly had the task of buying bread each morning. Each morning, right as the sun came up, Molly would leave the orphanage and walk a little over a mile to Mr. and Mrs. George's Bakery.

Mr. and Mrs. George were a sweet old couple who provided the orphanage with free loaves of bread. Molly took two loaves each morning from the sweet old couple and then took them back to the orphanage. Miss D's Orphanage was the smallest in all of New York City and therefore had quite a small number of girls. Miss D had precisely thirty-three girls under her care.

Miss D made sure each girl was up by seven, finished with their morning chores by eight, breakfast was done by nine, and then they had the rest of the day to do whatever. However, you must be back to the orphanage by seven at night because Miss D would close the doors by seven-fifteen. Then each girl must be done with their night chores by eight-thirty and lights out by nine sharp. Of course, Miss D was a kind lady, until she wasn't. She really did care for the girls, just not like a mother or father.

Each morning Molly would wake bright and early. Before the sun came up and before anyone else, she would get her chores finished. Molly found it easier to work in the silence and the darkness. It was also much better to concentrate without anyone yelling or screaming at each other.

Then, she would leave at seven to go get bread. Molly would climb out of her window to leave. Miss D kept the doors locked until she woke up, which usually wasn't until eight-thirty. However, Molly enjoyed being able to see the sunrise from her second story window. Molly enjoyed her days though. Even though they may seem dark and sad, Molly thought otherwise.

She would spend her free time exploring the big city. Molly loved exploring all of the different alley-ways. And little Molly had all day to do so. However, since Molly was one of the older ones, Miss D expected more of her. Molly had her share of being sent to bed with no dinner. One night Molly came home too late and Miss D had already closed the doors. Molly was forced to sleep outside. It wasn't that bad though. Molly tried never to do it again, but sometimes she got lost and couldn't help it.

Even though Molly had dark times in her life, she always tried to focus on the bright side. Even though Molly's circumstances were somewhat negative, she always tried to be positive. The only thing that kept Molly going was her dream. Her dream to have a home. And young Molly was determined.

CHAPTER 2

On the morning of November 10, 1941, Molly left earlier than usual to get to the bakery so she could see Mr. and Mrs. George. It was a highlight as Molly considered Mr. and Mrs. George her friends. Perhaps her only friends.

When Molly arrived, she sat and talked with Mr. and Mrs. George for quite some time before she had to leave. Halfway back to the orphanage, she realized she had forgotten to get the bread, so she had to go all the way back and pick up some bread.

When she told them she had forgotten the bread, Mrs. George selflessly got a loaf and gave it to Molly Grace. Molly pulled out of her pocket three dollars she had saved up over the years. She breathed and with a smile handed her the money. Of course, the old couple refused, but Molly Grace left the money on the table.

She stepped happily onto the sidewalk and began to walk back towards the orphanage. When she stepped through the door there, it was ten thirty in the morning. Since she was so very late, she was sent to her room for the rest of the day with no food. The girls at the orphanage had a way of sticking together, though, and they took turns taking food up to Molly. Molly was very grateful, but she would quickly snatch the food and eat it.

When Molly's favorite girl at the orphanage, little 7-year-old Shily Green, snuck food into Molly's room, Molly told Shily what she was going to do. Molly revealed to Shily that tomorrow morning, bright and early, Molly would go to get the bread, but really, she was leaving. Molly said she was getting too old to sit around and that she wanted to live her life. Molly was going to leave and go to Hawaii.

That night Molly packed her backpack with some clothes and hid it underneath her bed. When everyone was asleep, she snuck downstairs to get some food. She stuffed her backpack full of whatever she thought was needed. Then she went back upstairs and drifted off to sleep. The next morning, Molly woke up at 5:00 am, so she could leave. It was still very dark out and none of New York was awake.

She climbed over to the window that was in her room. She glanced behind her and then climbed out. She felt the brisk and cold air bite at her face. She walked towards the bakery. When she got there, she quietly knocked on the door. No answer. She began to knock a little louder. After a few seconds, Mr. George came to the door still in his nightgown.

When he opened the door, Molly said goodbye. Mrs. George came right behind Mr. George and Molly affirmed a goodbye to the both of them. They said they wouldn't tell anybody where she was going, but if someone asked them, they wouldn't lie. Molly thanked the old couple for being there for so many years.

Molly knew in her heart she would most likely never see them again. She didn't tell them exactly where she was going, but she shared that it was far away. When Molly left the bakery, she sprinted out of the city. Her excitement focused on exploration as her heart pounded with fear. Her mind screamed, "I'm scared to leave," knowing that once she stepped out of the city, she couldn't go back.

Molly caught a ride in a dump truck to carry her out of the city. When she got to the end of the city, she jumped out. Luckily it was still early in the morning so there was no traffic. For the very last time, Molly stared at the city she had called home for so many years. She then turned and walked into the wilderness.

Several hours passed since Molly's feet left the concrete

jungle. *It is probably noon,* she thought. After Molly got off the dump truck, she sprinted into the woods. She had been traveling through the woods for quite some time and she had no idea where she was going. She hoped she could get to Pennsylvania soon. She knew that once she was out of the city, they would quit looking for her. Molly was hoping to find a road because she was sick of the woods. The city girl was deep in her spirit.

A couple more hours passed by and still no road. Molly had been all day without food. She did have some water she packed. Molly could tell the sun was going to set soon. Molly needed to get out of the woods. She began to run, even though everything in her body told her to sit down. She ran for a long time, until she fell down trying to catch her breath. She reluctantly, but also quickly, pulled out her water bottle and drank a few small sips.

The sun was starting to set, and the last thing Molly wanted was to get caught out in the woods at night. She had heard all the stories of brave or foolish people who had gone in the woods at night never to return. So, she kept moving.

She was running when she heard something. She stopped and looked around. She could smell freshly cut wood. Out of nowhere, a tree was falling straight toward her. She began to run but didn't make it in time. The darkness closed in around her. Her eyes shut, and they stayed that way for a long time.

CHAPTER 3

Molly heard voices. She was on some kind of piece of wood. The voices moved closer. She reached to touch her head and felt a bandage. She slowly opened her eyes. She sat up and looked around. She could see tables and chairs. She was in a tent. Molly thought, and then it hit her, she knew where she was. She quickly jumped up and ran to open the tent flaps. Sure enough, she had walked into a lumber camp. Her stomach grumbled as she smelled the fresh eggs and bacon. The tree must have fallen on her. She must have slept all night.

She breathed in a sigh of relief. She was content, until a grouchy old man came up to her. He yelled a couple things in her face and she only stood there. When the old man finished, Molly asked where she was. He told her at a lumber camp. She realized he wasn't going to be much help. She walked around carefully until she found a young boy. She walked up to the boy and asked where she was.

"You're at the edge of New York. Pennsylvania is only four miles in that direction,"the young boy said. Molly thanked him and began to walk off.

"Uh, hey," the boy began, "What are you doing out here?"

"Well, I, I was only going for a walk when I got lost, and…….it was, um, getting dark, yeah." Molly said.

"That ain't true. You're running away," the boy smirked. Bam! He had figured it out.

"That's not true!" Molly unconfidently said back to the boy.

"Um, yeah it is. Look at your clothes, your shoes, your backpack." the boy replied.

"Ok, well, maybe it is true, but you better not tell nobody," Molly said, inching closer to the boy.

"I ain't going to tell nobody," the boy declared laughing.

"Good, well, goodbye, and thank you," Molly said as she slowly turned around to walk away.

"Hey, wait up," the boy said, calling after her. He ran and began to walk with her, "So, where ya headed?"

"That's my business and my business only," Molly replied rudely.

"Ok, where ya from?" the boy asked as they strolled back to the tent. Molly stopped walking and turned to face the boy. For a moment she thought she recognized his brown wavy hair and tan skin but instantly pushed the thought from her head.

"Uh, don't you have some trees to cut down?" Molly asked him because she wanted to get rid of him.

"No. I cut trees in little pieces. I don't cut them down," he said. Molly simply turned back around and began to walk again.

"Could ya please tell me where you're going?" he asked her once more.

"Why should I?" Molly asked as they walked in the tent.

"Cause' maybe I could help ya, and it's November 1941 in the state of New York," he said, giving her a sandwich.

"Um, ok, but how could you help me?" Molly asked him as she sat down and began to eat the sandwich.

"Well, I've been through these woods so many times. I know them like the back of my hand," He sat next to her and then lowered his voice, "I might also be trying to get away," he whispered.

"Really? Where?" Molly looked him in the eye.

"A little place I call home," he said with a smirk as he pulled out a brochure from his jacket pocket. Molly stared at the brochure with disbelief.

"You're joking!" she exclaimed.

"Nope," the boy answered matter-of-factly waving the Hawaii brochure, "That's my home, and I'm going there."

CHAPTER 4

Molly couldn't believe what she was hearing. She was completely caught off guard. She sat in disbelief wondering what she was going to do. She couldn't just leave the boy knowing he was going to Hawaii also. *Maybe it might be good to have some company*, Molly thought.

"So, where are you headed?" the boy questioned, putting his wrinkled and stained brochure back in his jacket pocket.

"I, I," Molly stammered, but the words would not finish..

"Ok....," the boy chuckled.

Molly pulled herself together, "I just, I don't have to tell you where I'm going,"

"Well, I guess you're right," the boy said. He stood and began to walk out. Molly sat still and watched him walk away. She knew she had to do something.

"Wait, I, I can't believe I'm telling you this, but I'm also headed to Hawaii," Molly exclaimed. Laughing, the boy turned around..

"I know, you're an awful liar," the boy said laughing.

"What, but, how?" Molly asked.

"When I said I was headed to Hawaii, you almost passed out!" he observed.

"Well, I guess you have a point. So, now you know. I guess you're coming with me," Molly uttered as she gathered her things.

"Only if you'll let me. I know traveling alone is always

easier, but I really need to get there," he said.

"Ok, pack your things. We can leave tonight," Molly said as she wondered what she got herself into.

"Great. After dinner, meet me in the main tent. By where Mr. Ed stays. We can get a little extra help from his money box," the boy said. Molly just stood there. She didn't plan on stealing anything, but she might have to. The boy smiled and then turned to walk out once again.

"Hey," Molly called after him, "What's your name?"

"Danny, I'm Danny Monte. What's your name?" he questioned.

"Molly, Molly Grace," she announced as the two finally shook hands.

Molly strolled around the camp until the sun began to set. She walked until she found a little place where she could have peace and quiet. When the sun turned the sky purple and red, she walked back to the main tent. She was with Danny at dinner, and they ate. It seemed as though everybody there had forgotten that Molly was still at the camp. However, they probably didn't care. The men there were stinky, tired, and they wanted to go home to their families. Quickly and quietly Molly and Danny devoured every morsel.

After dinner the two went their separate ways. Once everyone was in their beds and asleep, Molly Grace went to the main tent where she found Danny. When she saw him, she wondered why she ever agreed to allow him to come along.

They walked out of the main tent into the cold dark air. Danny tapped Molly on the shoulder and pointed to where Mr. Ed slept.

"No!" Molly whispered.

"Why not?" Danny asked.

"Because, that's stealing. I'm a runaway, not a thief," Molly confidently declared and walked on. Danny peeked back at Mr. Ed's tent and shook his head. When they finally set off on their journey, it was brisk and dark 3:00 a.m. The reason they started so late was because the men at the camp didn't turn off their lights until 1:30 a.m. and Molly and Danny left half-an-hour to ensure that everyone was asleep. When the two were out of the camp and almost to Pennsylvania Danny stopped walking.

"You've obviously never been a runaway before," Danny assumed. He plopped down and opened his water bottle.

"Yeah, I haven't," Molly said, rolling her eyes. Danny drank a couple big gulps of water.

"Um, we aren't even in Pennsylvania yet. Don't drink all your water," Molly demanded, sounding smart. Danny just smiled and put away his water bottle. He stood and began to walk again. The two walked in silence until 4:30 a.m. when they came across a road. There was a sign that read, Hattie's Pennsylvania INN, One Mile. They stopped. It was still dark out so it was likely that no one would be traveling. Danny looked both ways and began to walk on the road.

"What are you doing?" Molly inquired following him.

"I'm walking," Danny replied, walking down the middle of the road.

"Why? We should be going through the woods, where we'll have a better chance of NOT getting caught," Molly said looking around.

"Aw, come on. If anyone was out at this hour, they'd be silly. Besides, if we hear a car we'll run," Danny said as he kept on walking. Molly took a deep breath and realized that this was going to be a long trip.

Molly and Danny walked for a short while until they saw a little town in the middle of nowhere. They began to walk in the woods taking each step with caution. Even though it was still dark out, they didn't know who might be lurking around.

Eventually they came to Hattie's Pennsylvania INN and Diner. There appeared to be some commotion inside, but nothing much. They looked at each other and then opened the door. When they walked in, they discovered a woman working in a kitchen in the back. There was a couple talking quietly at a booth. Then, they got a glimpse of a man who was sitting at a table all alone. He wore a brown coat, brown hat, brown boots, and had a big brown bag. The two guessed he was traveling.

They sat at a table and picked up a menu. Molly gawked at the pricing and wondered why they came in there. The prices weren't awful, but Molly's funds were limited. The woman gracefully came out of the kitchen and gave the couple some coffee and biscuits. The two thanked her, and then they walked out of the building. She then came to Molly and Danny and a deep country accent left her mouth.

"What can I get you two sweeties?" She pulled out a piece of paper and looked at Molly and Danny.

"Yeah, can I have some eggs and bacon?" Danny said, setting his menu down.

"Of course, Sugar. What to drink?" She asked as she wrote down his order.

"Just water," Danny said. Then the lady looked at Molly. Molly froze.

With nervous butterflies in her stomach, "Um, the same please," Molly finally eked out.

"Coming right up!" the lady yelled as she walked back into the kitchen and cracked some eggs. Molly looked at Danny who simply smiled and leaned back in his chair.

"What are you doing?" Molly uttered under her breath. She was careful not to disturb the man in the brown coat. He had his hat covering his face, so she reckoned he was asleep.

"I'm ordering me some breakfast," Danny said quietly.

"We don't have any money," Molly reminded him.

"You don't, but I do," Danny snickered. Molly just stared at Danny and shook her head. After a few minutes the lady came back and gave them their food. She then pulled up a chair as if she were an old friend and began to talk to the two.

"So, where you babies headed?" She asked as she pulled out a cigarette and lit the thing.

"Um, we're just passing through. Our parents live not far off," Danny responded confidently. Molly stared at him in disbelief.

CHAPTER 5

A half-an-hour ticked by, and the lady was still talking to Molly and Danny. Danny had created an elaborate story of Molly and Danny's lives. Molly couldn't believe what Danny was imagining. He blurted lie after lie.

"And that's when we found Molly here," Danny said, gesturing to Molly, "My mama just couldn't help it. She always wanted a daughter, so we adopted Molly Grace," Danny said.

"Oh, my. That is so amazin'!" The lady said who was obviously fooled by Danny.

"Isn't it just that," Molly mouthed glaring at Danny. He just smiled and, in his mind, he was triumphantly patting himself on the back.

"Yeah, it's all great, but our Daddy fell ill two weeks ago, and he hasn't been able to work. Now we are running out of food. Mama sent us here hoping we could get something to eat. Mama hasn't eaten in almost two days. She's been too busy caring for daddy," Danny dropped his smile and put on a very sad face. Molly's expression stayed the same, however.

"Oh dear, you poor things. Here, take some food over to your folks. Let me get you darlings a basket," the lady said as she stood up and went to the kitchen. Danny just sat back and winked at Molly. Molly looked around and noticed that they were the only ones in the restaurant. The man in the brown coat was gone. Molly suddenly felt sick in her stomach. Something wasn't quite right.

The lady came back with a whole basket full of food. She gave it to Danny and then wished them good luck before strolling back to the kitchen. Danny stood up and peeked into the basket. It was filled with apples, bread, sweets, bacon, and cheese. Danny licked his lips and then began to leave.

"Danny, we have to pay," Molly stated.

"Um, no we don't," Danny said as he walked outside. Molly reluctantly followed him.

"Come on Molly. We have to get out of here. People are probably still looking for us," Danny said as he walked down the steps and onto the dirt road. He looked both ways and then began to run. Molly rolled her eyes and jogged after him. They didn't stop until they were far into the woods headed deeper into Pennsylvania. It was around 7:00 a.m., and Molly stopped walking. She felt they were deep enough into the woods for Molly decided that Danny's games had gone too far.

"All right, look, I get that you probably know more than me in running away," Molly said, and Danny smiled, "but you chose to come along with me. Therefore, you will listen to me and what I say. You might be so good at lying, but that is something I forbid you to do. We might be runaways, but we are most definitely not thieves or liars," Molly voiced, standing straighter and taller. Danny just looked at her. He opened his mouth as he was going to say something, but a twig snapped close by. They were being followed.

CHAPTER 6

Molly glanced at Danny who looked back at her. They stood still waiting for something to happen, but nothing did. Until out of the bushes came the man in the brown coat, the man for the diner He looked up and Molly and Danny could see his bright blue eyes. They all stood there waiting for someone to make the first move. But nothing happened.

"Can we help you?" Danny asked the man. The man looked at Danny.

"I know who you are. You're runaways," the man declared. Molly looked at Danny. They had been caught.

"Yeah ok, but what do you want?" Molly asked.

"You're the girl who ran away from the orphanage," the man remarked as he pointed to Molly, "And the Boy Thief," the man pointed to Danny. Molly wondered what the man meant, but she didn't worry about it. All of a sudden, people began to come out of the bushes. They surrounded Molly and Danny.

"Aw, stop it. Tommy," a lady said, "you're scaring them," Molly and Danny looked around in total confusion.

"Look kids, we're here to help you. Ok, we're all runaways," The lady announced, gesturing to all of the three people. Molly and Danny stood silent.

"Usually they fall right in love with us," The lady mumbled under her breath, "How about this? I'm Shelly Crane, and you are?" Molly looked at Danny whose expression changed from startled to disbelief.

"You're Shelly Crane? The Shelly Crane?" Danny awed. Molly had no clue.

"Sure am kid. Who are you?" Shelly Crane asked, "Well, actually I know who you are. You're The Boy Thief. You know you're pretty famous to all of us," Shelly finished. Danny blushed and laughed.

"Um, The Boy Thief?" Molly began.

"Oh, yeah that's me," Danny replied. Molly opened her mouth, but Shelly cut her off.

"And you must be Molly? The feisty runaway from New York," Shelly said. Molly peered at her with a hard glare.

"You know, you both are very famous. Or not famous but wanted," Shelly began, "You got a bunch of people looking for you guys and a big buck reward on your heads, but luckily, me and my people don't want money. We want more people, more people in our gang," Shelly said.

"Your gang?" Molly asked.

"Yeah, you haven't heard of us?" Shelly questioned while others snickered.

"I have!" Danny said. Shelly smiled and put her arm around Molly.

"Sweety, we are the biggest and baddest gang of runaways on this side of the country!" Shelly declared confidently.

"Oh, how lovely," Molly mumbled.

"And we'd like you two monkey fellas to come and join our gang. Come with us to our safe house, The Runaway Cabin," Shelly said. Danny looked at Molly, who shook her head.

"Sure, why not?" Danny said smiling.

"Well, Danny, we have a plan, and-" Molly began.

"Oh, please, I insist," Shelly said with a big toothy smile.

As they quickly and cautiously trudged deeper into

Pennsylvania with a bunch of strange people, Molly wondered what they were doing. They walked for what seemed forever, and then they went into a cave. Or a simple hole that had been dug. They walked through the hole, underneath the ground as if it were a tunnel. For an obvious man made tunnel, it might have been considered impressive because it was one mile long. They walked and walked in utter silence until a door finally appeared at the end of the tunnel.

"Welcome to the Runaway Cabin," Shelly said as she opened the door to a wonderful place. It was filled with music, food, and dancing. Tons of people were happily talking and laughing. Danny grinned as a bunch of people came up to him and asked for autographs and stories.

"This is where we live. We have over a hundred people who ran away from many different things. They're welcome here all their life or until they decide to move out. People come here from all over and the funny thing is, the police can never find us," Shelly shared with Molly as she gave her a tour. A big, six-and-a-half-foot tall man covered in tattoos strutted over and growled at Molly.

"No, no, Bim, that is not how we treat our guests. Say hello to Molly," Shelly insisted.

"Hi," the big man spoke, but his voice was no deeper than a six-year-old girl and no louder than a mouse. Molly giggled a little which made the big man, Bim, run off in tears.

"Oh, it's ok. He's very sensitive. Just keep walking around and make yourself at home," Shelly said as she ran after Bim. Molly glanced around and wondered. She imagined for a second she could stay here, but then she remembered her journey. She was going to Hawaii, with or without Danny, The Boy Thief.

CHAPTER 7

That night everyone gathered around the thirty-foot table to eat with Danny and Molly. Shelly toasted them. Everyone cheered. Molly had never been more welcomed in her life. Same with Danny. But something was off. Even though everyone was so happy and cheerful, Molly didn't know how these people could live with themselves. They hid underground their whole lives. Running from their fears of being caught.

Molly knew there was no way she could stay here. That night, she packed her things. While she was packing, Shelly popped up to her bunk bed.

"So, you're leaving?" Shelly asked. Molly turned around a little startled.

"Look, I know it would really be something for me to stay here. I'd have good friends, a place to stay where people actually want me, but I can't spend my whole life hiding from the real world. There are places I'm going to see, and I can't see them if I'm underground. I have to get to Hawaii. I hope you understand," Molly said. Shelly nodded her head.

"You're really something else, kid. I know it took courage to say that. I understand," she said. Then she gave Molly a journal.

"I'm giving this to you so that way you can remember every detail of your trip," Shelly said and then she walked out. Molly stuffed the journal in her backpack. Once all of Molly's things were packed and she was ready she went to Danny's room. She knocked on the door and he opened it.

"What?" Danny asked.

"Look, I'm leaving. I'm going to Hawaii. You're welcome to come with me, but if you steal or lie, that's it, you're done. I'm willing to give you another chance, but I'm leaving now," Molly said confidently. Danny stepped into the hall and closed the door behind him.

"Stop treating me like a baby. The only way I've survived is by stealing and lying, and if you think I'm going to give up my way of life for some little girl hoping to fulfill a dream, well then think again," Danny demanded. He vigorously opened the door and walked into his room. He then closed the door.

"So, are you coming or not?" Molly asked. Of course, she was talking to a door, so no one, or nothing answered. Molly shook her head. She then walked down the steps into the kitchen. She found Shelly Crane talking with someone. Molly waited. After Shelly was done, she went up to her.

"Um, how do I get out of here?" Molly asked.

"Follow me," Shelly said, leading her up a staircase. The stairs went on and on until they came to an attic. Up in the attic were many old trinkets. Books, coats, pictures. At the very top were more stairs that led to a door. Shelly opened the door. It led to the outside. But it was already 8:00 p.m. and a storm was thundering in. Molly decided it would be a great idea to wait until morning.

It was a long night, and Molly hardly got any sleep. She stayed awake thinking about where she would go. The next morning when Molly walked downstairs at 4:00, the only people in the kitchen were Shelly, Bim, and Tommy (the man in the brown coat). They had already prepared a bag of food for Molly because they had a plan.

"Right now, you're sixteen miles into Pennsylvania. Hawaii is a very long way off. I have train tickets that will bring you to California, all the way across the USA. Today you will board a train and head to Indiana. There you will switch trains and head to Nebraska. However, you'll have to stay in Nebraska for a day because the next train heading to Utah won't board for a day after you get to Nebraska. Once you get to Utah, you will then board a train to Nevada. There you will have to stay two nights, but you can stay at another Runaway Cabin, just tell them that Shelly Crane sent you. Then in two days' time, you will board a train that will get you to the west coast, on the edge of California," Shelly finished. Molly was overwhelmed, but there was still more to come.

"Once you're on the West Coast, there will be a man called Mr. B. Red. He owns a travel boat that takes people across the ocean to Hawaii, but he also has a way of helping runaways. Tell him that you know Shelly Crane," Tommy said.

"They won't let you board without an adult, so that's where Bim comes in," Shelly said. Molly started to laugh because she knew what they were going to suggest.

At 5 a.m. she was ready. They all walked up to the attic and stepped outside.

"There is a train station two miles in that direction. You must board the train at 5:30 a.m.," Shelly said. Goodbyes were exchanged before Molly and Bim walked through the woods, until they saw the train station. Bim then fixed his makeup up, for he was dressed as a lady. He had on a gigantic hat and a ginormous dress.

"This is so embarrassing," Molly could hear Bim saying in his quiet little voice. They both took deep breaths and then walked up to the train station. They skipped the ticket buying part, but they had to be checked by a conductor. He made sure Molly and her so-called mother were together and then let them on the train. Just before the train began to move, Bim snuck off.

Molly was alone. In a big world. In November of 1941. She stuck her chin out when she looked around and acted as if she belonged there. When the ticket man came to fetch her ticket, she gave it to him, and he took it with no questions asked. Molly was able to eat foods she had never even seen before better yet tasted. A lady said it was going to be a whole day before they reached Indiana. So, Molly got comfortable, knowing it was going to be a long trip.

CHAPTER 8

It was dark outside. By now Molly had been sitting down on the train for almost twelve hours. Though she still had five hours left, the only thing she wished was to be outside and standing. 5:30 p.m. rolled around, and Molly was starving. She saw other folks getting excellent food, but they had to pay for it. Molly looked around for a cheap meal. She knew she had food in her bag, but she figured she should save that in case she ended up having to walk.

Out of the corner of her eye, Molly saw a young girl headed to the trash can with a plate of food. Molly stood up and walked slowly over to the girl. The young girl, who was probably ten years old, had on a fancy dress and curls in her short blonde hair.

"Hey," Molly said, "Are you going to throw that out?" Molly asked, gesturing towards the plate that had a piece of bread, some chicken, and asparagus on it.

"Um, yes," the girl said unsurely.

"Well, if you don't want it anymore, could I have it?" Molly asked the girl. The girl looked at Molly, glanced over Molly's shoulder toward her parents, and then the young girl gave Molly the plate and walked off without saying another word. Molly smiled and went back to her seat.

Molly began to eat the piece of bread very quickly, but then she remembered that she was supposed to eat slowly, so as to look rich. As Molly was eating, a young man, probably eighteen, came and sat by Molly.

"Hi, I'm Nathan," the boy blurted as he stuck his hand out for Molly to shake it. Molly shook his hand with a mouthful of chicken.

"I'm Molly," Molly voiced once she had swallowed her chicken.

"So, why are you going to Indiana?" The man asked as he pulled out a sandwich. Molly was caught off guard and she didn't know what to say.

"I, um, I don't know, why are you going to Indiana?" Molly asked him.

"Ha, you're a runaway aren't you?" Nathan said as he took a bite of his sandwich.

"Wh- No," Molly said. Nathan just stared at Molly and raised his eyebrows.

"Ok, well, I've got family who lives there. My home. I was born there, ya see," Nathan said. Molly shook her head and in his bag, Molly noticed a small box, a ring box.

"You got a girl?" Molly asked. Nathan stopped eating and looked at Molly.

"You're very observant," he said as he closed his bag, "And yes, her name's Ally. I'm going to propose to her when I get back," Nathan smiled.

"Aw, that's so sweet," Molly commented, grinning. For the next two hours, Molly and Nathan talked. Molly had never felt so relaxed and happy in a long time. Around 7:30 p.m., Nathan went back to his seat a couple rows behind Molly. Molly decided to get some sleep while she could.

Molly woke up and saw the stillness on the train. It was almost 10:30 p.m. and no one was awake, except the conductor and workers of course. Molly looked up at the big clock and saw that she only had thirty minutes left in her train ride. She smiled and was glad it was almost over.

Molly looked out the window and looked at Indiana. Molly watched the quiet terrain and she liked how peaceful it was. The lights were off in the train so she could see fairly well outside. The train passed little farms and lots of land. Molly stayed still and quiet looking out the window until the train conductor came out of the main train car and began to announce something.

"It is currently 11:00 p.m. folks, and we are about to arrive at our destination in Blackford, Indiana. Please wake up and prepare your things for departure, thank you," the man said. Then, he returned back to the main train car.

Molly was already awake, but she glanced around her seat to make sure she had everything. She had everything. She was ready to go. Of course it took about five more minutes to pull into the station, and then Molly stood up. Molly and Nathan walked off together and stopped in front of a large sign. They stared. Molly saw her next train to Nebraska, which would leave in thirty-minutes. It was just about the same time at seventeen hours long.

"Well, I guess I better get going. My dad is over there waiting to pick me up. It's been a pleasure Miss Molly. Good luck on your journey," Nathan said.

"Thanks, good luck on your proposal," Molly responded smiling. Nathan left, and Molly, again, was alone in the train station as a clock struck 11:15 p.m.

Molly headed to a bench. It would be the perfect place to park and watch the clock as it slowly turned every sixty seconds. Molly waited and waited. She sat alone with no one else around except the man working and an old lady. Five minutes clicked by, and the old lady came over to Molly and sat down on the bench beside her. Molly smiled at the old lady and sat still.

"Where are you headed young missy?" the old lady asked.

"Nebraska," Molly replied.

"Aw, you've family there?" the old lady asked. Molly opened her mouth as if to reply, but out of the corner of her eye she saw a young figure walking toward her. The young boy had brown wavy hair, tan skin, and looked a lot like Danny.

Molly squinted her eyes, so she could see him better. It felt like it took hours for him to get to Molly. However, he was there before she knew it. Standing in front of her with a confused expression on his face.

CHAPTER 9

Danny began, "Look, what I did was wr-"

"Wrong. Yeah it was. You slammed the door in my face. Then you chose not to come along." Molly felt lost for words. Danny took a deep breath, and Molly prepared for whatever sarcastic comments would follow.

"I'm sorry," was all Danny mustered out. Molly stared at him with a hard glare for what felt like five minutes. Her glare softened with each second, and she was thinking deeply. She noticed the clock read 11:25. Her train was going to pull into the station at any minute.

"Look, I know you want nothing to do with me," Danny began, and Molly raised her eyebrow, "But, I promise I'll do better. I'm not that good at apologies, but please Molly, I need to get to Hawaii," Danny said as the train pulled in and people began to get off. Molly didn't know what to say, so she stood up with her bag and stuck her hand out for Danny to shake it. He shook her hand.

"Well, that was just beautiful!" the old lady exclaimed before clapping her hands and smiling from ear to ear.

Together - Molly and Danny boarded the train at 11:30 headed for Nebraska. There were plenty of empty seats, so it was very quiet. At 11:45 p.m. the ticket man came to collect the tickets. Molly gave him her ticket, however Molly didn't know if Danny had a ticket. Molly's heart skipped a beat when the ticket man asked Danny for his ticket. Danny smiled and pulled out a ticket and gave it to the man.

The man took the ticket and smiled. When the man was done he left. Molly and Danny sat in a row without saying a word. By midnight they both fell asleep. When they woke up at 9:30 a.m. there was a breakfast lady offering free breakfast snacks. Of course Molly and Danny took whatever they could and then ate it or stuffed it in their backpacks. The conductor announced they would be arriving at around 4:30 p.m. So, Molly and Danny got comfy because it was going to be a long ride.

Molly and Danny both stayed quiet until noon when the lunch lady came around once more and gave out food. Danny grabbed a ham and cheese sandwich and Molly took one also. As they were eating their sandwiches Molly couldn't wait any longer and she just had to ask Danny.

"Danny, what happened after I left that morning?" Molly asked Danny. Danny looked at Molly and then into the air space in front of him.

"Oh, well, that whole night I couldn't sleep cuz' of what I acted like, and so I thought about it a lot, and I decided that going to Hawaii was more important than anything they had at the Runaway Cabin," Danny paused, "So, that same morning you left, I left also. I followed you and Bim to the train station and then boarded. I was originally going to sneak on, but Bim saw me after you got on and he gave me tickets. He said that they knew I was going to go too," Danny finished. Molly just shook her head and then turned back toward the window.

A couple minutes later Molly pulled out her journal and opened it. Inside she read a note, *No matter where you go or whatever you do, never forget who you truly are -Shelly.* Molly smiled at the encouragement. She flipped through the pages and was amazed at how calm and fresh the journal seemed. She wanted so badly to write in it, but it was so captivating just how it was that it took great strength for Molly to decide to write in it.

However, when she went to begin to write in the journal, she realized that she had no pencil. Molly hunted around for a pencil. She slowly stood up so she could see if anyone on the train had an extra pencil. She couldn't see anything though. She casually strolled out of their little compartment of two seats, past Danny, and into the aisle. She then strolled the aisle towards the restroom. However, as she was walking, she looked and looked for a pencil, but no one had one.

When she got to the restroom, she reluctantly walked into the room with a smell that was rotting her nostrils. When she thought she had been in there long enough, she walked out, back down the aisle toward their seats. On her way, she kept looking. When she was almost to her row, she saw the man in front of them was taking a nap and seemed to have fallen asleep with a pencil in his hand and a paper in the other. She gingerly walked over to him and took the pencil cautiously out of his hand. She looked at the man's briefcase, which had the name Richard M. Nixon in big bold letters. The only thing that passed through her mind was, *what a weird name.*

Molly walked back to her seat and sat down pulling out her journal. She looked at Danny who was staring at her.

"So, who's the thief now?" Danny asked her, crossing his arms.

"I didn't steal it. I borrowed it," Molly replied, preparing to write. Danny stood up and leaned over the seat and looked at the man Richard M. Nixon. He sat back down and shook his head.

"That man looks fancy. I bet one day, he'll be famous and he won't have his lucky pencil to help him," Danny said.

"I doubt it," was all Molly muttered. She began to write things down in her journal, including a letter to Mr. and Mrs. George. She wondered how their bakery was and how they were.

After a while Molly put away her journal because her hand was hurting. She slowly stood up and slipped the pencil in

Richard M. Nixon's hand. A couple minutes after the pencil was safely back in his hand, he woke up. It was around 2:00 in the afternoon, and most people were napping.

"So, what's the plan?" Danny asked.

"Well, when we get off in about two hours, we're going to have to find somewhere to stay and then in the morning we'll board a train going to Utah," Molly said.

"Ok," Danny replied. It was then silent for a few moments.

CHAPTER 10

"So, Molly, what's your full name?" Danny asked. Molly looked at him trying to find out if he was being real, but the only thing she could see was a young boy who was trying to make friends.

"Um, Molly Grace Ford. Yours is Danny Monte, right?" Molly replied.

"Yeah, my parents never gave me a middle name," Danny stated feeling a little sad.

"Who were your parents?" Molly asked.

"Well, my mom was a nurse in World War 1 while my dad was a sailor in the Navy. They first saw each other in the hospital. My dad got hurt. I'm not really sure how, and my mom was the nurse who took care of him. Eventually, they fell in love and got married. They had me in 1925 in Tennessee. I was only seven when my dad left. My mom couldn't take care of me anymore, so she sent me to an orphanage in Virginia. I ran away, got caught, and then was sent back to it. I did that for a whole year until I ran away for good to Pennsylvania. There I stayed in hiding. I would steal things, just to keep myself alive. I even made a society with other kids. We were called The Takers, well, because we took things. I was the leader. They called me the Boy Thief. After a bit, I left that and went to get a job. I worked at the lumber camp for a whole year. I was thinking of leaving, and then you showed up. When you said that you were going to Hawaii, I knew that was it.

My chance," finally taking a breath, Danny finished.

"Wow, you've had it rough, huh?" Molly asked. Danny just shrugged his shoulders.

"Your turn," Danny said. Molly glared at Danny.

"I don't really know much about parents. My dad fell in love with mom and then she got pregnant and had me. Shortly after I was born though, she left. She went to become famous or something. My dad stayed with me and we lived in our little house on the edge of New York City for as long as I can remember,"

Molly paused, " However, when I was little, my dad got murdered by some psycho-path. We were at a bank and there was a robbery. He told me to go hide somewhere, so I went into a closet, and then when I came out, everyone had been killed, including my dad. So, the government or something decided to send me to the orphanage. That's where I've been living the past six years. Almost seven," Molly finished.

"Sounds like you didn't get it much better, huh?" Danny asked. Molly just shrugged her shoulders. It was silent for a couple moments.

"So, how old are you?" Molly asked Danny, trying to change the subject.

"Sixteen. What about you?" He replied.

"I'll be fifteen in five days," Molly said.

"Really! Well, that's great! So, your birthday is November 18?" Danny asked.

"Thanks and yeah," Molly said laughing because she was surprised at his enthusiasm.

Molly was a little amazed at how much she was enjoying her conversation with Danny. She never knew he could be so nice. She glanced at him and saw that underneath his blue eyes, brown wavy hair, and his tough personality, he was really just a sweetheart.

"Why are you going to Hawaii?" Danny asked her, interrupting her thoughts.

"Oh, um, I don't know. I heard about it and saw some pictures. People say it's a paradise, so I think I just wanted to see for myself. Also, I wanted to get away from the orphanage," Molly finished smiling. She looked at Danny waiting for him to say why he was going to Hawaii.

"At the lumber camp, I heard some men talking about the Naval Fleet that's there at Pearl Harbor. Our Naval Fleet. They said that you could work in the Navy and get paid and stuff. So, I'm going to join the Navy, like my father," Danny said. Molly just shook her head in approval.

CHAPTER 11

The two stayed silent until 4:30 when the dinner lady came around. They both grabbed something to eat and then packed their things. As they pulled into Lincoln, Nebraska, they noticed how flat the land was. They both hopped off the train and walked around the train station for a bit. They saw a big clock that read 5:54. It was going to be dark soon so they stood outside of the train station looking at the city of Lincoln. They saw very few cars, but many wagons.

Molly and Danny had no clue what to do. As they stood there, a man rode up in a wagon. He had on a dusty hat, a long jacket, a long beard, and big brown boots. He stopped in front of Molly and Danny.

"Are you the Beconny siblings?" the man asked. Molly looked at Danny who tilted his head.

"Why yes, we are," Molly said. Danny began to scratch the back of his head and he looked at the ground.

"Well, then, whatcha waitn' for? Hop in," the man said, showing what's left of teeth underneath his big beard. Molly and Danny reluctantly got in the back of the wagon.

"What are you doing?" Danny leaned over and whispered in Molly's ear. Molly looked at him and shrugged her shoulders. They rode in the wagon for at least an hour, and it was far past dark when the bearded man stopped in front of a big mansion.

"Well, here's ye stop," the man declared. Molly and Danny

hopped out and starred with their mouths open at the gigantic house. They stared at the massive columns and many flowers. Without warning the bearded man drove off and left Molly and Danny standing there unsure of what to do.

A few minutes passed and Molly and Danny still stood in the cold darkness at the front gate. A lady soon opened the front door and yelled something into the house. Then a short chubby man walked out of the house toward the gate. He unlocked it and then motioned Molly and Danny inside the yard.

"We have been expecting you children. With the death of your father, Madam Marine's brother Joe, you poor things had nowhere to go," The chubby man said. Then he walked up the drive way toward the front door. Molly and Danny stood still however.

"Well, come now kids, it is very cold out," the chubby man turned around and said. Molly and Danny looked at each other. Danny tilted his head as Molly shrugged her shoulders and walked on up the sidewalk toward the big white house.

The sidewalk was rather long. It had too many flowers to count lined up along the side. Even though it was dark, Molly and Danny were both overwhelmed by all of the colors. When they got to the front step, the chubby man ran up and opened one of the massive front doors.

"Oh, you poor darlings!" A middle aged woman ran out and tightly hugged both Molly and Danny. "Come inside, come come," the lady continued as she practically dragged Molly and Danny inside.

Immediately, the smells of chicken, turkey, rolls, fruits, vegetables, and cakes, flooded Molly and Danny's nostrils. They both relaxed in the warmness of the home.

"Oh, dear, Sydney, come show Avery and Ana to their rooms," the tall skinny lady expressed to the short chubby man, Sydney. With his hands behind his back, Sydney nodded and came to the tall lady.

"Come children," Sydney called. He led them up a massive staircase to a hall that had probably twelve rooms in it. At the end of the hall, there was another staircase.

"Avery, here is your room," Sydney motioned toward Danny as he opened a door and inside was practically a whole other house. Danny walked inside slowly and dropped his bag on the floor. He stood awe-struck until Sydney showed Molly, or Ana, her room which was right across from Danny's. Molly walked into the massive bedroom. She had never seen anything like it before. It had a huge window with even bigger drapes that were covered in flowers.

She walked over to her bed, which was also covered in flowers. Her bed was so huge that it took a lot of muscle to climb up on it. When she was up on it, she laid back and on the top of the bed, there were pictures of little naked angels with harps. She stared at them in total confusion. She sat up and realized that she was getting mud all over her clean bed.

She climbed down and ran over to a massive closet. When she opened the doors, there was every kind of clothing in there. She stepped back to get a full look at all of the clothes. She grabbed some brown pants, and a brown coat. When she was changed she looked in the ten foot tall mirror. When she was satisfied with her look, she walked over to the humongous window. She looked out of it and could see the driveway. After a few moments, a car pulled in and out walked a tall man, in a black suit, with a stern expression.

CHAPTER 12

Molly ran across the hall over to Danny's room. She found him looking at a picture.

"Danny, look out your window!" Molly said urgently as she ran over to Danny's window and opened his massive curtains. Danny walked over and looked at the man in the black suit.

"Who's that fancy fella'?" Danny asked. Molly let go of the curtain allowing the room to become dark and she lowered her voice.

"That's Ivan Gualy. He's trouble, Danny. He came to the orphanage twice in New York City. He takes kids to different orphanages across the U.S. He's even taken kids from their homes cause the kids were either failing in school or acting badly. He's probably here to take us, Avey and Ana, to an orphanage," Molly finished.

"Well, what do we do?" Danny gasped, "Do you think he'll recognize you from New York City?"

"I don't know, but we need-"

"Children," Sydney's voice interrupted their conversation, "come down here!"

Danny and Molly looked at each other and then walked out of his room and down the large white steps. Molly and Danny walked slowly into the dinning room where the man, Sydney, and the tall lady were standing.

"Aw, hello children. I am Ivan Gualy. I heard about the death of your father and came right away to take you things to an orphanage," Ivan said. Then he took out a piece of paper and asked the tall lady to fill it out.

"Are you sending us to an orphanage?" Molly leaned over and asked Sydney who was standing beside Molly and Danny.

"I'm sorry, you poor things. Madame Marine just can't take care of you. She thinks you all will have a better chance at an orphanage," Sydney finished with a sigh.

"Avery, come here boy," Ivan said. Danny put on a brave face and walked over to him.

"How old are you, child?" Ivan asked.

"Uh, twelve," Danny guessed. Ivan nodded his head and then motioned for Molly to come over.

"And you Ana?" Ivan asked her, glaring hard into her brown eyes.

"Um, eleven," Molly also guessed. Ivan squinted his eyes at her almost as if he was looking into her soul.

"Are you sure?" Ivan asked.

"I, uh, yes?" Molly replied a little shaky.

"Uhm, it says here you are ten," Ivan said pointing to a number on a paper.

"Um, my little sister gets confused sometimes. You see sir, she'll be eleven in a couple months…. and she also likes to trick people," Danny said standing beside Molly. Ivan glared at Molly and Danny.

"It says here that Ana's birthday is not until February. It is November young man," Ivan stood up and glared harder. Danny swallowed a big gulp of fear. It was silent for a moment until a knock on the door startled everyone.

Sydney walked and opened one of the big front doors to

two young children and a tall man.

"Come in," Sydney said. The tall man and two children stepped inside.

"I am Bartholomew, Joe's friend. I have his two orphaned children, Avery and Ana," The tall man finished with a hand on each of the children's shoulders. Molly and Danny tried to back away, but Ivan's stare stopped them.

"Hold it right there. Who are you then?" Ivan pointed a long skinny finger at Molly and Danny piercing right through their invisibility. Molly and Danny froze. Then, they grabbed their backpacks from a chair and took off running. They ran right past everyone and right past Ivan's yells of demands. They ran out the front door, down the steps, through the yard and pretty flowers, and right through the gate.

Molly and Danny sprinted as fast as they could away from the big house. They ran down the street and heard the sound of an engine car starting. They glanced at each other before they were blinded by the car's lights. Together they rushed off the road and into the woods. They both raced for quite some time until they could no longer hear the cries of people and the sound of cars.

At the same moment they sat down gasping for air. Molly looked around in the darkness of the night and wondered where they were. She slowly stood up.

"Where do you think we are?" Molly asked Danny without looking at him. When a couple seconds passed and he didn't answer, Molly looked at him. Danny stood up and stared at Molly with his hands on his hips still trying to catch his breath. Danny still looked at Molly with a plain expression.

"What were you thinking?" Danny finally said.

"What do you mean?" Molly asked, coming closer to Danny so she could see his face.

"Molly, you lied, and now they're onto us. What were you

thinking?" Danny repeated.

"I, I don't know. I just, I guess wanted some excitement?" Molly replied unsure.

"Look, you told me that I can't lie or steal things. And now you are," Danny said.

"What, I didn't steal anything!" Molly cried back.

"The clothes, Molly,"

"We are borrowing them......" Molly finished.

"No, we aren't, and you know that. Molly, make up your mind. Are you going to be a good runaway or a bad one?" Danny asked her.

"Ok, look, I-" All of a sudden they heard voices off in the distance.

"We'll finish this later. Let's go," Danny said. Quietly, they both took off running headed away from the voices. Molly and Danny hustled as fast as they could until they spotted a shallow wide creek . They both stopped wondering if they could avoid the icy water, but torches and voices coming closer changed their minds.

Danny darted across the icy water without a twinge from the cold. He got to the other side and turned and waited for Molly. She scrambled across as fast as she could without slipping and falling. The icy water stung her feet and when she got to the shore, they were practically numb.

Despite the numbness, the two kept moving. Twisting and turning as little as possible, they fled through the woods. The more they ran, the closer lights got. They stumbled out of the woods and onto a farm. They noticed a little log cabin, a barn, and a house. They both ran toward the barn and opened the door and climbed inside.

Hurriedly Molly climbed up a ladder to the hayloft with Danny right behind her. They lied down and covered themselves up in hay. They stayed quiet for a couple minutes, and then they heard it. They heard the voices of men and the barking of dogs. How Ivan got so many men so quickly, they couldn't figure it out.

They listened as two or three men pushed into the barn. One man climbed the ladder and started shuffling hay around. Miraculously, Molly and Danny were never found. When the men found nothing and were unsatisfied, they left the barn and continued searching outside. It felt like forever until Molly and Danny noted silence. The men must have left - either gotten tired or continued on somewhere else.

CHAPTER 13

After close to an hour of silence. Danny uncovered himself from the hay. He stood up and looked around. Molly uncovered herself from the hay and stood as well.

"What are you doing?" Molly asked him.

"You said the train leaves for Utah in the morning. Then we need to get going," Danny said.

"What about the men? What if we get caught?" Molly asked.

"We just have to hope that we don't," Danny replied as he climbed down the ladder. Molly asked no questions because she knew she had made a mistake, so she let Danny take the lead.

When they reached the bottom of the ladder, they walked out of the barn cautiously and quietly. Danny walked toward the house. Molly called after him in a whisper, but he wouldn't stop. Danny walked up the steps and knocked on a front door. There was no answer. Danny knocked again. There were some noises inside the house and then the door began to open. A lady stood with the front door open and there was flower in her hair and on her apron.

"Can I help you?" she questioned, then three young children came up and stood behind her.

"Yes, uh, could you point us in the direction of Lincoln city?" Danny asked.

"Sure, it's-" The lady began before she was cut off by a man's voice.

"Who's at the door, Sherry?" The man said.

"Just some kids," Sherry replied. Then there were footsteps and the man showed up at the door. He put a hand on his wife's shoulder and he had a soft expression on his face.

"Can we help you kids?" the man said. He had a firm but soft voice.

"Uh, yes sir, could you please point us in the direction of Lincoln city?" Danny asked once more.

"You headed there?" he asked.

"Yes sir," Danny said.

"Well, I could take you kids in my wagon. It'll take me a minute to get it around, but I'll have you both in Lincoln City in probably an hour and a half," The man said.

"That would be wonderful sir," Danny said, elbowing Molly.

"Uh, yes, thank you," Molly replied as well.

Finally, the man pulled around in his wagon. Molly and Danny climbed in along with two other children, an older boy and a younger girl. The kids sat in the back and the man was in the front seat steering the two horses.

"So, who are you guys?" the little girl asked.

"Maybell," the boy said, pulling the young girl, Maybell, into his lap. Danny laughed and eyed Molly.

"Well, I'm Danny, and this is Molly," Danny told Maybell.

"I'm Maybelll and this grumpy guy is John Jr.," Maybell said. Danny, Maybell, and John Jr. all conversed, but Molly remained silent. She stared at the stars and couldn't help but become in awe at the magnificent site.

Molly felt awful. She wondered why she did what she did.

She made a mistake, and it was extremely costly to Danny and her. Luckily, they found a sweet family who helped them. Danny and Molly had the whole night to get back to Lincoln city. They would board the train at eight tomorrow morning. Molly got comfy because it was going to be a long bumpy ride to the city. Even longer than the first wagon ride.

CHAPTER 14

It had been a while now since they left the sweet family's farm and hit the road to Lincoln city. It was most likely around eight o-clock by now. They had driven for about forty-five minutes now. Maybell was asleep, and John Jr. was having trouble keeping his eyes open.

Danny crawled over and sat by Molly. Molly still stared at the stars though.

"Are you ok?" Danny asked her.

"No," Molly mumbled.

` "Why not? We have the best transportation in town," Danny said.

"Yeah, and we probably would never have had to bother this sweet family if I hadn't screwed up. I should've just kept my mouth shut," Molly replied. A few moments of silence followed.

"Look, so you screwed up. It happens. But, you can't let it bother you, or else the rest of your life you'll be so focused on the past and what you did then, that you won't be able to live in the future," Danny said.

"Well, thanks Mr. Poetic," Molly replied smiling.

"And besides, if you hadn't lied to the bearded man at the station, then we probably would be in a dark creepy alley right now. You just have to look on the bright side," Danny told her.

"Ya know, Danny, I have to tell you, you're not so bad," Molly replied.

"Thanks, you're not so bad yourself," Danny said back. The two rode in silence for the rest of the wagon ride.

Molly looked around and everyone in the wagon, except Mr. John, was asleep. Molly continued to gaze at the stars and she was still amazed at how they lit up the sky. Then she heard something. She looked straight and then to the sides and backwards. She squinted her eyes and looked at the tree line to her right. She could hardly see anything in the darkness of the night, but she knew something was there.

"Hey, Mr. John, did you hear anything?" she asked him.

"No, no I have not," Mr. John shared with Molly without turning around. Molly still looked toward the tree line, and she thought she saw a man. However, as quickly as she saw the figure, it had disappeared even quicker.

"I thought you and everyone were asleep," Mr. John said. Molly just smiled. She grabbed her backpack and searched through it. She was looking through her backpack to find her journal, when she realized; it was gone.

Molly was caught off-guard. She didn't know what to do. She didn't know where to look, or how to look. She never had much, so she wasn't really used to losing things. She tried to be quiet while she searched around in what little space she could. She retraced her steps, in her mind, to remember where she last had it.

The last time she had it out was on the train, but the last time she saw it..........was at the mansion. She remembered watching it fall out when she took off her backpack to lay on the huge bed. Oh great, she thought. It probably slid underneath the bed and was laying there all alone.

So, Molly decided to try to get some sleep. There was about thirty minutes until they reached Lincoln City, so she figured she could at least shut her eyes. However, as soon as Molly closed her eyes, Maybell woke up. She sat up and rubbed her little eyes. Then she woke John Jr. up. And of course, then Danny woke up. They were all awake and so they started a conversation and Molly joined in so as to keep herself awake.

"So, Molly, what was it like being in an orphanage?" Maybell asked Molly and John Jr. nudged Maybell.

"Uh, well, I wouldn't say it was the funnest time of my life," Molly said.

"Did you get fed?" Maybell asked her.

"Maybell," John Jr. said.

"What?" Maybell replied.

"I mean, yeah, it wasn't like I was starved or anything," Molly told her.

"What about you Danny?" Maybell asked him.

"What about me?" Danny asked Maybell.

"What was it like in your orphanage?"

"Uh, well, I didn't like it," Danny told Maybell. Maybell just nodded her head and looked at the ground.

"I have a mamma and a daddy," Maybell blurted out.

"That's good," Danny and Molly both said, ending with a laugh.

"Hey kids, we're coming up on Lincoln City, so get your things ready," Mr. John finally spoke. Making sure they had everything, Danny and Molly sat up straight so they could see around Lincoln City. The lights were ever so bright and there were smells of food and flowers.

They rode through the streets for about fifteen minutes before they pulled up on the train station. Molly and Danny both hopped out and put their back-packs on.

"Thank you so much, sir. It means an awful lot," Molly

said to Mr. John.

"Yes, thank you," Danny also told Mr. John.

"Aww, it was my pleasure. You kids are fun to have around. Stay safe now," Mr. John said as he climbed back in the wagon. As Molly and Danny waved them off, they could hear Maybell and John Jr. saying bye.

The two run-a-ways walked up the big steps into the train station. Although it was eight-thirty at night, the station was still busy. So, Molly and Danny walked around until they found a corner. Molly sat down in the corner. Danny lied on a bench nearby. Before Molly could even get comfy, she dozed off.

CHAPTER 15

"All aboard!" the loud man cried at seven-fifty six the next morning. The loud noise startled Molly and she jerked awake along with Danny who fell off the bench a couple feet away.

"Danny, that's our train!" Molly vigorously stood up. Danny slowly stood from his fall and rubbed his eyes. He yawned, quickly gathered his things, and they were both walking toward the big train.

"All aboard," the man repeated even louder. Molly and Danny both kept a steady pace towards the big black train. They had to wait in a short line before they boarded.

Molly and Danny hurried onto the train and found a seat. Since this train was much larger than the last one, it had its own little compartments where four people could sit. So, Molly and Danny walked into one. Across from them was a lovely old couple. The woman who was dressed in a long fur coat had a warm expression on her face. She sat by the window staring at the station. The elderly man beside her pulled out tiny reading glasses and then pulled out a large newspaper and began to read.

"All right folks, our trip today will last about twenty hours. So, that means get comfy. Our schedule says we will arrive at the next station at about four a.m. tomorrow. Thank you," Then the man's voice was gone.

Molly and Danny got comfy. Molly sat by the window and watched as the train station slowly disappeared as they rolled out of Lincoln City. It was quiet for the next thirty minutes. Until the old lady asked Molly a question.

"So, what's your name sweety?" the old lady asked.

"Oh, um, I'm Molly, Molly Grace," Molly replied, turning away from the window to face the elderly couple.

"And you?" The lady asked Danny.

"I'm Danny, Danny Monte'," Danny said.

"Nice to meet you both. I am Alice Stone, and this is my husband, Gerald," She said, patting her hand on his shoulder.

"Uh, yes dear?" Gerald asked her slowly, lifting his head from the newspaper.

"Oh, nothing dear. It's just there are these two wonderful kids here," Alice said.

For the next two hours, Molly and Danny listened to Alice's stories. They tried to keep awake, for the old lady was a sweetheart, but poor Alice had an awful slow voice. Danny even fell asleep for a couple moments. When, finally, Mr. Gerald tapped his wife's shoulder.

"Alice, why don't we go take a walk through the train?" Gerald asked her, standing up and holding out his hand.

"Well, all right, I'll be back dearies," Alice claimed as she and Mr. Gerald walked out of the compartment, closing the door behind them. Then, silence followed.

"What a sweet lady," Danny said, rubbing his eyes.

"What do you mean, you were asleep," Molly giggled.

"Yeah for like three minutes,"

"No, no, more like an hour, Danny," Molly stated.

"You missed the part when Alice's daughter wore her fancy dress and then fell in the creek and ruined it. You also started snoring when Alice said that her mom died, but the funeral got canceled. So, I nudged you and jerked up," Molly said practically laughing.

Danny sat with his mouth hanging open unsure what to say. As quickly as the old couple left, they were back. Molly and Danny enjoyed their company though. When Mr. Gerald and Miss Alice were settled in their seats, Alice started up again.

Going on and on about how she had a dog named Tots and how he was the best dog ever. Alice said she knew Tots ever since she was six years old. However, at the end of the story, Alice said that when she was twelve her father finally told her that Tots wasn't a dog; Tots was a turtle. Danny and Molly couldn't help but laugh along with Mr. Gerald and Miss Alice.

"So, why are you two going to New Mexico?" Alice asked them. Molly and Danny didn't know what to say.

"I'm sorry, New Mexico?" Danny asked.

"Why yes dear, that's where this train is headed, isn't it Gerlad?" Alice asked and Gerald shook his head up and down as he read a new newspaper.

Molly and Danny just looked at each other.

"Is something wrong? Are you two okay?" Alice asked Molly and Danny. Molly and Danny still stared into each other's eyes not needing to say anything. Danny licked his lips and turned slowly to Miss Alice's face.

"Yes Mam, we're okay," Danny said as he sank down shortly after being copied by Molly.

The two stayed silent wondering how they boarded a train headed to New Mexico. Eventually noon arrived, and everyone was hungry. The lunch lady, or ladies, came around with trays of food and served everyone. Molly and Danny ate some sandwiches but were very distant from the real world.

CHAPTER 16

"Gerald and I are going to go walk around for a bit. We'll be back, dearies," Alice said at one. Danny and Molly smiled, but said nothing. When the old couple was gone and the door closed, the two began.

"How did we board a train to New Mexico!" Molly cried.

"I don't know!" Danny exclaimed, standing up in confusion.

"I mean, they checked our tickets right? At the door they checked them, and we got through," Molly said.

"I know," Danny replied, walking in circles.

"What are we supposed to do?" Molly asked.

"I don't know!" Danny cried sitting back down. "I don't know Molly," Danny kept saying while moving his hands through his hair. A few minutes passed before Danny spoke again, "I mean, we just have to wait until we get there and then decide. We might have to hitchhike to California."

"We can't hitchhike to California, Danny," Molly said trying to laugh, but Danny just looked at her.

"Then what do you suggest we do?" Danny asked.

"I don't know, I don't know. I guess we're just going to have to wait until we get there," Molly said. Danny nodded his head and then Mr. Gerald and Miss Alice came back in and sat down.

"Well, that was fun," Miss Alice declared as she got comfy.

"You know, children, Gerald and I were walking around, and we heard some people talking about the war. Did you know that there is a man, by the name of Adolf Hitler slaughtering thousands of Jews in his country?" Alice said. Molly recalled hearing something about this.

"Well, I actually saw something about him in a newspaper," Molly said.

"Yeah, me too," Danny responded. Then Alice leaned in.

"You know, some think that America is going to join the war," Alice said and then sat back up.

"Well, what do you think?" Danny asked.

"I believe that we will go to war. Japan and Germany hate us and something might happen," Alice said.

"Oh, come now Alice," Gerald said looking up from his newspaper, "We aren't going to join the war," For the next thirty minutes, Alice informed them of what was going on around the world. Thankfully, soon after, Alice and Gerald went on another walk.

Molly looked at Danny who just glanced back. Molly had heard bits and pieces of what was going on, but she had no clue of how serious it was.

"That's why I am going to join the Navy," Danny said. Molly stayed silent for the next couple of hours. Eventually Alice and Gerald came back, but as soon as they sat down, they both fell sound asleep. Most of the people on the train were napping. Molly had time to think about what they were going to do when they got to New Mexico. What was going on in the world. And whatever happened to her journal.

It was around three-o-clock. Danny and Molly once again sat with Alice and Gerald listening to Alice ramble on about anything and everything.

"And then, do you know what happened next?" Alice asked Danny and Molly. Molly shook herself awake.

"No ma'am, I don't," Danny replied, rubbing his eyes.

"Well, my sister and I decided to put paint in her bonnet. Oh, she got so mad and we got in so much trouble. Though, she never messed with us again," Alice then paused and took a big breath.

"We're headed to New Mexico because my son and his fiance are getting married there, for some reason, but I am very excited!" Alice said and she clapped her hands together.

"Oh, well that's nice," Molly said smiling.

"Did I ever tell you two the time that my older brother and I put ink on my teacher's chair?" Alice asked, "Well, it all began when our old teacher left and we got a new teacher. The kids in the schoolhouse were not happy. Now, back then I was quite the fire-cracker, and I didn't stand for her. She just hated kids, I tell you. Well, one day....." Alice's voice began to slowly fade away as Molly entered her own world.

As Molly thought over the last couple of days, she couldn't help but think about all of the little details of her and Danny's journey. Mr. Ivan, from the government. Sydney, the butler. The man in the woods on the wagon ride. There were so many things to think about and Molly felt she couldn't think about every single thing. So, she decided to write in her journal. However, when she reached in her bag, she remembered that it was gone

Her only guess was that it was underneath the big fancy bed at Madame Marine's enormous mansion. Luckily she never wrote anything really important there. Even though Molly and Danny had many pleasures and rode in style, they were still on the run. If they got caught by Ivan, or someone else like him, they could be sent to different parts of the country to awful orphanages. Molly had realized that Danny and her had gotten too comfortable because they were letting details slip that could give away their freedom. Even though Alice and Gerald were a sweet old couple, Molly and Danny needed to be careful.

"And I said, that's what I said!" Molly heard Alice say as Molly slowly began to come back to the real world, "But no, she still didn't believe me. So, later that day, Joshua and I snuck into the school-house and put ink all over her chair. Of course the next morning it dried, so we snuck in very early and put ink all in her bag, her chair, her desk; it was everywhere!" Alice said as she began to laugh.

"Oh, you remember that Gerald," Alice asked.

"Yes dear," Gerald replied as he once again was reading a different newspaper.

"What did I miss," Molly leaned over and asked Danny. However, Danny did not move but his eyes were open. Molly nudged him and he shook.

"What, what?" Danny asked, rubbing his eyes.

"Ha, you were asleep," Molly laughed.

"I was not," Danny said, but he began to laugh also.

CHAPTER 17

At last five-o-clock rolled around. The dinner ladies came and offered food. As Molly and Danny devoured ham and potatoes, they noticed how Alice seemed so distant sometimes and yet so close other times.

Danny and Molly couldn't help but feel nervous as they got closer and closer to New Mexico. Molly was still baffled that Danny and her got their tickets that had Utah on them checked and yet somehow they still managed to board a train headed to New Mexico. Danny and Molly decided that the man who was checking their tickets wasn't really checking them and therefore they were able to board the wrong train.

Through the whole dinner that evening Alice stared out of the window aloof to the rest of the world. By the time Molly and Danny were finished with their desserts, Alice was back to normal and talking non stop about the silliest things. Alice went on and on about everything from how the sky reflects the ocean and that's why the sky is blue to how the stars are like lightbulbs. Molly and Danny tried their best not to laugh, but the elderly lady's presumptions just didn't seem to add up.

"It's getting late dear, why don't we go for a walk?" Gerald asked Alice at seven-thirty.

"Well, all right dear," Alice said, standing up to hold her husband's hand and then they both walked out and closed the little door behind them.

"So, what do you think we're going to do," Molly broke the silence.

"I, I don't know Molly," Danny said standing up.

"Have you ever been to New Mexico?" Molly asked Danny.

"No, you?" Danny replied.

"No," Molly paused, "Uh, Danny, on the wagon ride over, I saw someone in the woods,"

"And?" Danny said.

"Well, he was watching us. I think he was spying on us," Molly said.

"Maybe," Danny replied.

"Do you think that Ivan put him up to it?" Molly said.

"What?" Danny said, almost laughing.

"Look Danny, Ivan and I don't really agree," Molly began, "He wants me dead."

"You can't say things like that," Danny sat down making his voice quiet, "And he doesn't want you dead,"

"You don't understand, he does. Ivan is an evil man. He's mental. You have to trust me Danny. We're being followed," Molly snapped back.

"Ok, well, why does he want you dead then?" Danny asked.

"Because he-" Molly was cut off by the startling opening of the little door and the return of Alice and Gerald. Danny took a breath.

"We'll finish this later," Danny whispered to Molly.

"Did you two know that today is November 14, 1941?" Alice asked Molly and Danny as she settled down.

"Yes Mam," Molly said.

"Did you know that we have made so many advancements in technology, and well everything!" Alice said excitedly.

Molly and Danny just smiled. Danny was quiet and Molly could see the gears turning in his head. He was pondering hard on many things. Molly felt bad for not being able to tell Danny the whole story, but she would tell him, just not now.

Danny watched as the scenery slowly changed into desert. He stared out of the window looking in any direction. It was dark out so he couldn't see much, but he still watched. Molly listened to Alice's stories until eight-thirty when Gerald pulled out a tiny pillow and asked everyone to be quiet. Alice smiled and said goodnight. Shortly after both Gerald and Alice slept like rocks.

Molly took a deep breath and relaxed in the darkness. The stillness of the train comforted her. Even though the people on the train were quiet, the train moved quite loudly through the night air.

Molly had heard stories of the desert. People would get so burned, exhausted, and dehydrated. She heard of the mirages and hallucinations that people experienced. She just hoped that Danny and she wouldn't have to suffer through that.

Molly was awakened by a loud noise. She couldn't tell what the noise was, only that it frightened her. The noise kept getting louder. The noise sounded as if something was dying. Molly looked around in the darkness. As she listened to the noise more, it wasn't as frightening, just annoying. Molly soon realized that the noise was Gerald's loud snores. When she realized this, she couldn't help but laugh a bit.

She slowly stood and stretched by reaching her arms up high and then out to the sides. She gently slid open the compartment door and decided to walk around the train. She checked the clock at the end of the hall and it read two-o-clock. That meant that they would be getting off the train in about two hours.

Molly walked as quietly as she could. She strolled past lots of people who were asleep. As she walked through the rows though, she once jammed her toe into a piece of wood sticking out of a door, and it took everything to keep from yelling out. She quickly grabbed her foot and sat down in a nearby chair holding her foot in her hand. She noticed a man asleep beside her. Soon the pain went away, and she slowly stood up.

As she stood though, a firm hand grabbed her shoulder and pulled her back down. A hand went over her mouth and a voice whispered not to scream.

"Uhuh, by lon't mean-" Molly tried to say with a hand over her mouth. The firm grip on her face soon loosened.

"I won't scream," Molly whispered unsure. The hand released. Molly couldn't see anything in the dark, but she could tell the figure that sat beside her was no small human.

"Listen up," A deep voice began to whisper and a cold knife was brought quite close to her face.

"You've got a bounty on your head little girl. Ivan Gualy, The Big Boss is willing to pay a whole lot for your head. So, here's what's going to happen, you're going to go back to your little compartment with your little friend, and then when we get off in two hours, you will see me at the train station waiting. You will come over quietly and nobody will get hurt. We will peacefully deliver you to Ivan so I get my money. Afterwards, we all live happily ever after, sound good?" the man finished.

"Um, no. Why does Ivan want me dead again?" Molly asked back.

"You know why. Now get out of here and forget that this ever happened," Even though Molly couldn't see his face well, she could smell the grossness of the man.

Molly swallowed and stood. She tried her best to walk casually back to the compartment, but she could feel her legs wobbling beneath her. She slowly slid the compartment door open and then turned to close it. She went and sat down trying not to breathe so loudly.

"Where were you?" She heard Danny ask beside her. Molly didn't say anything.

"Um, hello, anybody there?" Danny asked once more.

"Molly, what is going on?" Danny finally asked, sitting up and rubbing the sleep from his eyes.

"We have to get out of here Danny," Molly whispered.

"What?" Danny questioned.

"Danny, there's a man. He's working for Ivan, he's here to take us to Ivan, to get us killed. We, or I, have a bounty on my head. He was the man in the woods. We have to run Danny," Molly said in a very quiet whisper.

"Uh, what? Molly, what are you-" Danny asked her quite loudly.

"Shhhhh," Molly said, covering Danny's mouth with her hand, "Danny, this isn't a game. We're being followed by bad people. They will kill us. We have to do something," Molly removed her hand from Danny's mouth.

"Like what?" Danny asked.

"I don't know. He told me that we have to go to him when we get off and nobody will get hurt, but I don't like that idea," Molly replied.

"Yeah, me neither," Danny paused, "Maybe we could get off a different door than he does. Or we could run really fast. Pretend we don't see him. Act dead, ha that always works. We could leave with Mr. Gerald and Miss Alice. No, that would put them in danger," Danny kept going on a tangent.

"Do you think Ivan planned this, Danny?" Molly asked.

"Um, I don't know. I mean maybe. You must have done something really bad for him to want you dead Molly," Danny said.

"It's not what I did. It's what he did that I know about," Molly stammered so quietly, she could barely hear herself say it.

"What do you mean?" Danny asked in an even quieter voice. Molly looked at Danny in the darkness. She could barely see his blue eyes. Molly did not want to tell Danny what she knew. She knew if she told him then he would also have a bounty on his head and it would be her fault. However, the man knew about Danny, so Molly figured that it'd be better if Danny knew so Danny wouldn't be running from someone or something he didn't know.

"Danny, look, I was sworn not to tell anyone this, but I guess this is a life or death situation, so here goes. Danny, Ivan has done terrible things. He wants me dead because I know about them," Molly paused.

"Well, what has he done?" Danny's voice changed from happy to full of concern and ambiguity. Molly swallowed.

"He-" Molly was cut off by the sudden opening of the sliding compartment door. The man stood at the opening with a smile on his face. Molly knew she shouldn't have told Danny anything. Now not just she was in danger, but Danny too.

"Who are you?" Danny asked, standing up.

"Shh," The man put a finger to his lips. Then the man pulled out the knife and began to play with it. Danny tensed and then slowly sat back down knowing he would not win the fight.

"Who is he?" Danny asked Molly. Molly just shook her head. So, Danny sat back and pretended to get comfy even though anger and confusion were written all over his face. The man, with the knife in his hands, stood at the doorway blocking it.

CHAPTER 18

Molly felt horrible. She now put not only Danny in danger, but Gerald and Alice too. Even though they still slept soundly, if they had overheard anything or saw anything, then they could be wanted too.

Molly looked at the large man. He was probably six-three and he had wide shoulders. She tried to study his face in the darkness. The man was bald but had a short beard. She couldn't know what color though, it was too dark.

For the next hour-and-a-half the man stood at the doorway with the knife in his hands. Luckily, Alice and Gerald never woke. Danny and Molly thought long and hard. The last thing they wanted to do was fall asleep, besides the man's hard gaze was keeping them from doing so.

It was finally 3:30 a.m., so they would be exiting the train in thirty minutes. The man stepped into the hall and checked the clock. He grunted and came back and leaned on the door frame of the door. It was a few minutes before he spoke.

"Look, we'll be getting off in thirty minutes. So, when we do, you will find me in the train station. You will come to me, because well, it would be an awful shame if this knife slipped and landed on one of these lovely older folks right here," The man pointed the knife at Gerald and Alice.

"I guess your friend told you why you two will probably be dead in three days," The man snickered at Danny.

"No, she hasn't told me anything," Danny articulated. Molly could hear the anger in his voice.

"Sure kid, sure," the man said as he walked out, closing the sliding door behind him. It was complete silence for a couple of moments. Danny turned quickly to face Molly. She looked at him and even through the darkness, she could see the anger on his face.

"What was that?" Danny whispered intently. Molly opened her mouth, but nothing came out.

"Look Molly, I don't know what you did, or saw, but we came on this journey together. So you better start talking or we both are going to die and maybe more people," Danny licked his lips and took a breath, "I have no clue what's going on here, but that was not a good man and I am most definitely not going with him, I don't know about you."

"Of course I'm not going with him! I'd like to live another day thank you," Molly snapped back.

"Okay then, tell me why he wants you and me dead right now," Danny said, not joking around.

"Ok, Ivan-" Molly began but was once again cut off.

"all right folks. Sorry to wake you, but we are about to pull into Taos, New Mexico. So, please gather your things and get ready to get off. We hope you enjoyed your ride over, thank you," The man's voice stopped.

Even though Molly and Danny's conversation was once again unfinished, they both held their gaze. The lights of the train turned on, and Molly could see the frustration even better on Danny's face. Gerald and Alice stirred awake.

"Well, good morning," Alice said as she put her things into a little bag.

"Good morning," Molly replied, turning away from Danny. Molly forced a smile onto her face.

"Did you two sleep well?" Alice asked. Molly looked out of the window and shook her head up and down. Danny did nothing except look intently at the floor. It was very dark out and would stay that way for a couple more hours. Molly could only wonder what might happen in the next couple minutes.

Alice sat in her chair with her hands in her lap and her bag's handle around her wrist. Gerald, of course, sat with a newspaper in his hands. Molly wondered where he got all of his newspapers. He seemed to have an endless supply.

Because it was still completely dark outside, the lights were on in the train. This made it impossible for Molly to see anything out in the darkness. Eventually, the train pulled upon a little building, and Molly could tell it was the train station. There were lights on at the train station, so Molly had a better view of what was outside. Desert. There was only desert for miles and miles.

Molly remained hopeless. There was nowhere to run. Nowhere to hide. Her journey was turning into a complete failure. She had brought an innocent boy into the matter, and now, they were practically being dragged to their deaths all because Molly knew something that Ivan didn't want her to know.

Molly sat. Waiting. Watching. Listening. She waited for the man to walk by, but he never did.

"Are you two getting off?" Alice asked Gerald as she stood up and waited at the sliding door.

"Oh, um yes," Molly said with a smile. Molly stood and Danny got up too.

"Well, in case we get separated getting off, goodbye," Alice said hugging both Molly and Danny, "You two dears are both little joys. You made my ride so pleasant, thank you." Alice smiled before Gerald and Alice walked out into the hallway.

"What do we do?" Danny asked, shaky. Molly looked out

of the window to see Gerald and Alice slowly walk around the train station. And then she saw him. The man was leaning against the wall. He smiled at Molly and then casually put his hand on his waist moving his jacket to where the knife was hanging so Molly could see it. He then glanced at Gerald and Alice who had their backs turned from the man. He then looked back at Molly and tilted his head. When Molly did nothing, he took a step towards Alice and Gerald.

"We get off now, Danny," Molly said, quickly grabbing her backpack and walking out of the little compartment into the hallway.

"What are you doing, Molly?" Dany asked frantically following her. Molly stopped so quickly and turned around that Danny ran into her.

"Sorry," Danny said.

"Danny, the man, he's gonna kill Alice and Gerald if we don't come," Molly stated plainly.

"Then let's go," Danny nodded. They both practically ran through the small hallway. They ran out of the door and down the steps to where they reached the wood floor. Molly looked around to try and spot the man. Suddenly, Danny sprinted to her right. She didn't even think and followed him.

She soon saw what Danny had seen. The man was sneaking up behind Alice and Gerald. Though he snuck causally, if a person were to look closely, they would spot the long pointy knife sticking out of his coat.

Molly and Danny stopped running and moved to a fast walk. Molly glared at the man and he glanced at Molly and Danny and smiled. He backed away from Alice and Gerald and walked into the little train store. Molly and Danny reluctantly followed him into the little building. There was a bench inside and the man told Molly and Danny to sit on it.

They both sat down and glared up at the tall man. He was

blocking any way of escape and threatening to kill anyone. He stood with his hands on his hips in front of Molly and Danny.

"You chose the right choice," The man smiled showing some missing teeth surrounding by other yellow teeth, "For a moment, I thought you two were going to run."

"Believe me, it took everything not to," Danny said just as the man leaned in close to Danny's face.

"Don't be smart with me boy. I can kill you if I want. You don't have a bounty on your head, but since you were riding with this here young lady who does, I thought it best to bring you too," the man finished by scratching his bald head and then scratching his red beard. Molly glared at the man in disgust.

"What are you going to do to us?" Molly asked.

"Well, I'm going to hand you two over to Ivan and get my money," The man finished. He kept looking around afraid that he was being watched.

"Why does Ivan want us? Or her?" Danny questioned.

"Quit asking questions, boy," the man replied.

Danny glanced at Molly. They were both thinking of running, but even if they got away, the man would most certainly kill someone. The man knew that Danny and Molly didn't want anyone else getting hurt, so he used that against them. They waited there for fifteen minutes. The man saw someone pull up in a wagon and smiled.

"Come on," he said to Molly and Danny while pushing them to walk in front of him, "And if either of you try to run, someone will die."

CHAPTER 19

They walked out to a wagon where a Mexican man was sitting with the reins in his hands. The Mexican man sat with a smile on his tan face and a piece of hay in his mouth. When he saw who was walking towards him, he took the piece of hay out and his expression changed.

"What are you doing?" He asked the man who had the knife.

"Shut up, Antonio," Before the man with the red beard pushed Molly and Danny into the wagon bed he blind-folded them so they couldn't see where they were going. They climbed in and sat down on wood that was covered in sand. He slammed a board across the end of the wagon so Molly and Danny couldn't get out. Then the man with the red beard climbed on the seat bar beside Antonio.

"What-" Antonio began.

"Drive, Antonio, now," The man with the red beard said harshly. Antonio flicked the reins and they were off. They got onto a dirt road and rode for a couple minutes.

"All right, we'll stop here." The man with red beard said and jumped out, "We'll wait till morning to keep going. Tie them up," he finished.

"Yeah okay Austin," Antonio mumbled and jumped out.

"Come on," Molly heard Antonio say and then she felt a

hand on her arm. She slowly stood and walked.

"Stop," Antonio said and then he jumped down, "All right jump," Molly swallowed away the fear and jumped blind folded. Her feet reached the ground sooner than she expected and so she fell hard onto the sand.

She stood and waited for Danny. She heard him jump down, however he didn't fall.

"Sit here," Antonio said as he tied Danny and Molly's hands together, "We will wait until it's light out and begin again. Make any noise, and somebody might die,"

Molly found it funny how many times Danny and she had been threatened in the past couple of hours. Then Molly heard another body jump out of the wagon. And then another. She could feel someone sit down beside her. Then two more pairs of hands were tied to Danny's and hers.

Molly dared not to speak. She wondered who sat tied up with her and Danny. She wondered how Danny and she had gotten themselves into this situation. Molly knew they would escape, but she didn't know how or when. All because Molly knew something about Ivan, her journey was not turning out good and even worse she had put Danny in danger that he didn't deserve. He didn't even know why Ivan wanted her dead. She felt bad for not telling him, but she would; sometime.

Molly didn't get any rest during the three hours they sat on the hard ground. The air became quite chilly, but no one dared to utter a word. She was too busy thinking. She wondered about many things, such as who these people were and what was going to happen to them.

She didn't know if Danny slept. She also didn't know whose other hands were tied up with Danny's and hers. More than once she thought she felt something crawling up her leg. Molly did not like scorpions, or anything like that. So, she never really found a liking for the desert.

Molly recognized Ivan's secret. He was a bad but very powerful man. Ivan had an underground network. He, of course, was the boss. Ivan had men in different parts of the country. Molly didn't know how big his network was. She knew he had a lot of men helping him, but since he was hiding it from everyone, Ivan's network wasn't that huge.

Molly understood what he was. Who he was. She realized what he was doing. Of course, she felt horrible for not being able to tell anyone what he was doing, but there were too many lives at risk, including her's and Danny's and any friends Molly had.

Molly once knew a police officer. He patrolled the orphanage. One day, the police officer found out about Ivan, so he was going to tell the government. However, he couldn't get there in time. In the dead of night Ivan slaughtered him in cold blood.

Recalling that thought made Molly shiver. She was sworn not to tell anyone of Ivan's secrets. This was only one of hundreds of murders that Ivan had committed. However, no one knew about them except Molly, or so she thought.

CHAPTER 20

"All right, let's get a move on," Austin said bright and early at 7:00 a.m. Before Molly knew what was happening, she was up in the wagon and sitting on sand. Molly did not like sand that much. She found it unfortunate that she sat on some.

Molly didn't know how long she sat in the wagon. It felt like hours. They went over bumps, down hills, up hills, to the right and then the left. It seemed to Molly that they just might be going in circles.

She tried to listen to Austin and Antonio's conversation, but their voices were too muffled. She made out the words *hate*, *crazy*, and *Ivan*. Still, Molly had no clue who sat beside her. She hoped it was Danny, but there was no way of telling. With her hands tied and her eyes covered, she was practically hopeless.

Molly felt the heat on her face. Even though her eyes were covered, her whole face was hot . Which meant, sunburn. Quite a lot of sunburn. Molly guessed it was around eleven a.m. when the wagon stopped. It had been more than a couple hours since they started. Molly could only guess where they were.

When she slowly walked and jumped out of the wagon, she didn't fall this time, she heard no one else around except those in the wagon and those who were driving it, Antonio and Austin.

While Molly sat on the ground, Antonio took off her blind fold. Excitedly, she opened her eyes, but only found herself being blinded by a very painful light. Molly's eyes had been in darkness for so long that they needed time to adjust to the bright light of the hot sun.

Eventually, Molly was able to squint around and then she could open her eyes fully. Molly observed the wagon, Austin, Antonio, Danny, two other kids along with miles and miles of open range of nothing but sand and desert. She felt herself shrink beneath the many miles of an intensely hot misery.

"Hello everyone," Austin walked up and began to talk to the kids, "So, as you all know, you're going to be given over to Ivan, to most likely be killed, so I can get my money. You all know something about Ivan that he don't want nobody knowing. So, when you learn something that you ain't supposed to, there are consequences." Austin paused and then began to laugh maliciously. Molly noticed a big tattoo on Austin's wrist or was it a scar? Then Austin walked off without another word spoken.

"Sorry about that," Antonio came up and said, "He's just a little grumpy right now that's all."

"Who are you?" Danny asked.

"Antonio Eveylen," Antonio replied happily.

"Can you let us go?" Danny replied.

"No, I'm afraid that I can not do," Antnio, frowned.

"Well, why not?" Molly began, "We're just a bunch of innocent kids,"

"My dear, you know something about Ivan, and therefore the whole underground
is in danger," Antonio said, "This is how I get paid."

"By giving kids to Ivan so he can kill us?" Danny yelled.

"My boy, you make it sound so bad," Antonio responded.

"It is bad you dumbo!" Molly yelled. Antonio glared at Molly and then walked off.

Molly peeked around for any way of escape. She figured

that they would stay here until nightfall and then Ivan would come get them. So, they just had to slip away before then.

Molly glanced at the other kids. One was a boy with red hair and green eyes. The other one was a girl with red hair and green eyes also. They looked like siblings.

"What's your name?" Danny asked the boy.

"Luke," the boy replied.

"And you," Danny looked at the girl.

"Ruth," she said.

"I'm Danny."

"I'm Molly," Molly said, joining the conversation.

"How old are you guys?" Danny asked.

"We are almost fourteen," Luke replied.

"Are you guys related?" Molly couldn't help but ask.

"Yeah, we're twins," Ruth said.

"I'm sixteen," Danny told them.

"I'm almost fifteen," Molly said smiling.

"So you guys know about Ivan also?" Ruth asked.

Molly shook her head up and down while Danny shook his side to side.

"Wait, so you know about him," Ruth said, pointing to Molly. "But you don't?" she continued as she pointed to Danny.

"So, why are you here?" Luke asked Danny.

"Molly and I are traveling together. She apparently knows something about Ivan, so they just took us both," Danny replied.

"Oh," Luke said. Then Danny turned to Molly.

"All right, Molly, spill the beans," Danny said seriously. Luke and Ruth were messing with something and were not really listening, so Molly decided to tell him.

"Ok-" Molly began.

"Ok," Danny said back.

"Ivan is an evil man," Molly found her mouth saying.

"Yeah, I know this part, keep going," Danny inquired.

"Well, so he has an underground network," Molly hesitantly replied.

"Yeah, I figured that out, but what is he really!" Danny asked forcefully.

"He's a German spy!" Molly yelled. Austin appeared around the wagon and then disappeared again. Danny licked his lips and raised his eyebrows.

"Yeah," Molly said, taking a deep breath.

"Wow, he is bad," Danny said, "What do we do?"

"I don't know," Molly replied plainly.

"We have to escape," Danny said.

"Yeah, we agree," Luke joined in.

"All right, we have to somehow take these ropes off our hands and untie them from the wagon, but if we do, we have to be exceptionally quiet," Danny said.

"They probably have guns, and they aren't afraid to chase us down," Molly told them. Danny nodded.

"So, what's the plan?" Luke asked.

Danny, Molly, Luke, and Ruth discussed their escape for two hours. They stayed quiet but were all full of energy.

CHAPTER 21

Finally, when the hour arrived, they were ready to set their plan into action. It was two-o-clock. Neither Molly, Danny, Luke, nor Ruth had had any water or food for a while now, but they were ready to leave.

Antonio and Austin were sitting up in front of the wagon. It wasn't the smartest idea, leaving their prisoners alone at the back of the wagon.

There was a rock a couple feet away from Ruth. Since Ruth and Luke were tied to one side of the wagon and Molly and Danny on the other, Ruth was able to lift her left leg and reach it out as far as she could. So when Luke and Ruth sat down, Ruth was able to just barely reach the rock with her toe. She pulled the rock in and then somehow managed to cut the ropes off.

However, as soon as Luke got free, they heard horsehooves. Molly turned around to see a man on a horse riding hastily through the desert.

"Stop, stop. Go back!" Molly yelled to Luke and Ruth just before the man rode up. Luke and Ruth made it appear as though they were both still tied up. The man had on a hat and baggy clothes. He had a big bushy blonde beard and blonde ponytail. He wasn't too large, but he was tall.

The man with the bushy beard swung off his horse and then walked over to Antonio and Austin. They chatted for a couple moments, and then the three of them walked over to

Danny, Molly, Ruth, and Luke.

"I thought you said there was only two?" The man with the bushy beard turned and said to Austin.

"Right, well we picked up these two," Austin pointed to Luke and Ruth, "on the way. Funny story - they was at the station trying to tell people about Ivan,"

"Well, what am I supposed to do now?" The man with the bushy beard yelled.

"Right um well-" Austin stammered lightly.

"It's not like I have two horses!" the man with the bushy beard cried.

"Quit yellin' Joshua!" Austin said.

"Don't tell me what to do," Joshua replied. Entering into deep thought, Joshua put his hands on his hips.

"I got it," Austin triumphantly said, "We could kill a couple,"

"And why would we do that?" Joshua asked.

"So that way there wouldn't be as many," Austin replied. "It's not like Ivan cares. He was just going to kill em' anyway,"

"You do have a point," Joshua said. Austin and Joshua looked at each other and smiled. Molly knew what was coming. They were going to kill someone. Then they both took their mean-looking knives. However, as Joshua and Austin walked closer, Antonio bravely grabbed a board and striked both of the men on the head. Joshua and Austin fell down, unconscious.

Molly curiously tilted her head up and looked at Antonio, who was sweating uncontrollably. Nobody said anything until Anotonio stepped closer.

"What are you doing?" Danny asked.

"I'm helping you. Now, let's go," Antonio replied. Molly was in shock. She never expected this. She was sure that she or somebody else was going to die. When Danny and Molly were untied, they put Austin and Joshua in the wagon. It took everyone's help, but they eventually put the dead-weight in the wagon. Then they started back the way they came.

"Where are we going?" Molly asked Antonio. Luke and Antonio sat on the bench upfront, while Danny, Molly, and Ruth had the job of guarding Austin and Joshua.

"Back to Taos, there is a Police Station there," Antonio replied.

"Why are you helping us?" Danny asked.

"Because," Antonio stopped the wagon and turned around to face Danny and Molly, "It's the right thing to do," And once again, they were off into the hopeful hands of freedom.

CHAPTER 22

It was four-o-clock. The sun intensely beat down. Molly looked around at everyone's faces. They were red and burned. There was no shelter in the wagon from the burning heat. Water was running low. However, Molly and Danny had a lot of food stuffed in their back-packs.

Austin and Joshua had not awakened. *Antonio must have hit them on the head rather hard,* Molly thought. Molly tried to recall the last couple of days. Molly and Danny had traveled about half of the country. Molly started her journey on November 10, 1941. It was now November 15, 1941. Molly and Danny had been through a lot, yet freedom was not any closer. The Runaway Cabin had been revealed to them. Amazing people found a way to help them. Pretending to be "orphans," they went to a giant mansion. Narrowly escaping, they ran through the cold night air into a sweet family, who truly desired to help them.

Molly was amazed that she and Danny had not been captured or hurt. Well, eventually, Austin did capture them, but they were slowly getting away from him. With each step the horses took they became closer to the police station. Molly felt a little bit more hope. Hope that soon, Ivan would be behind bars for betraying his own country and all of his minions. Hope that Molly will be in Hawaii. Hope that Danny, Luke, and Ruth would get what they need. Hope that things would be made right and Molly would be free from the knowledge of Ivan's evil secrets.

But it was only hope. Hope was small compared to Molly's

circumstances. Hope is something everyone forgets about, especially Molly. Over the years, learning to accept the fact that no matter what happens, she would always get hurt. She had accepted her fate because whenever she did hope for good, it always ended up being bad. Molly looked at hope as a trick. A deceiver. A liar. A scoundrel.

"We have less than an hour now till Taos," Antonio said. Molly didn't know how much longer she could take the heat. Or anybody else. She just prayed that they would get to Taos soon.

"So, Antonio, how long have you worked with Ivan??" Molly asked.

"Long enough," he replied.

"Ok, that doesn't tell me anything," Molly darted back.

"Ivan took me in when I needed a home. Made me feel welcome. A year ago he told me what he was doing. I didn't agree. However, I had nothing else to do; I had nowhere else to go. So, Austin and I have been working here in New Mexico," Antonio shared with her.

"So, you betrayed your country to fit in?" Molly questioned.

"Look here young lady," Antonio whipped around, stopping the wagon, "This is not my country. I needed money. I needed food. Nobody else would hire me. I'm sorry that you and your people must deal with Ivan, but it's not my problem," Molly just stared as Antonio talked.

It was then quiet for a couple moments. Molly had learned a lot of things in the past couple days. She learned that there are good people and there are bad people in the world. She didn't know about Antonio yet.

"So, how did you and Luke get here?" Danny asked Ruth.

"Well, my brother and I have run away from many different orphanages. We've been on the run the past couple of months. We found out about Ivan at our last orphanage. When the adults didn't believe us, Ivan tried to kill us. So, we ran. We've been running ever since. However, yesterday, we got caught," Ruth said.

"So you're also orphans?" Molly asked.

"Yeah," Luke said, turning around to face Danny, Molly and Ruth.

"Our parents died in a boat accident. We never knew them," Ruth said.

"So, where are you guys headed?" Danny asked.

"California. There's a safe haven there for runaways," Luke said.

"We're headed to California, too!" Molly exclaimed.

"That's nice. Why are you going to California?" Ruth asked.

"Well, we're trying to get to Hawaii," Danny said quietly.

"Hawaii! That's so awesome!" Ruth exclaimed.

"What's the safe haven, Luke?"Molly asked.

"It's called the," Luke leaned over the bench and got real close to Danny, Molly, and Ruth, "Runaway Cabin. It's one of, if not the biggest safe havens there is,"

"Yeah," Molly agreed as she and Danny smiled.

For the next thirty minutes Luke, Ruth, Molly, and Danny all got to know each other really well. Luke was quiet, but smart. His flat red hair and green eyes said a lot about him. He talked when needed and was heard every single time. He was intelligent, practical, and used whatever resources he had to make something spectacular.

Ruth however, tended to use her mouth more than her brain. She would speak up quite often. Ruth's short bob cut and rounded face made her look younger than she actually was. Luke and Ruth had each other's backs. They would defend each other and back each other up.

After a long trip through the desert, they finally reached the police station. Danny and Molly hopped out of the wagon and raced inside. Inside, there was a large man with a bushy black mustache and jet black thin hair.

"Help, we need help," Molly cried to the man. The man tilted his head.

"Help," Molly said confused while using her hands to show him, "Uh, bad guy! In the wagon!" She pointed to the wagon where Antonio had tied up Austin and Joshua. The man had no expression on his tan face. Then his thick eyebrows went up, and shock was written all over his face.

When the man cried something in Spanish, four other men lunged from the backroom. Molly and Danny followed them outside where Antonio began to talk with the man in a language Molly didn't understand. Austin and Joshua were dragged out of the wagon. They were still unconscious.

The man looked at Antonio and smiled.

"Muchos gracias," the man said, then he and his men carried Austin and Joshua into the police station.

"Well, that's over," Antonio said with his hands on his hips. Everyone stared at the station door waiting to see if Austin or Joshua came out.

"What's going to happen to them?" Molly asked.

"Chief said that they would be held here until tomorrow and that's when the big police will come and get them. They will be questioned and then most likely held in prison for a while. Austin has been wanted for murder, so that's why the chief was very grateful," Antonio said.

"So, where are you going to go?" Danny asked Antonio while getting Danny's and Molly's back-packs from the wagon along with Luke's and Ruth's belongings. .

"Home. My mother lives in a place called Louisiana. I will go to her," Antonio said as he climbed in his wagon. He got comfy and then looked at Danny, Molly, Luke, and Ruth.

"It has been a pleasure, kids. I'm sorry I had to kidnap you. I hope you do well in your journeys," Antonio nodded towards each one and then flicked the reins. He rode down the dusty road with the four kids watching him until they got tired of watching.

"Now what?" Ruth asked, rubbing her eyes from all of the dust.

"We go to California," Danny said, looking at the sun.

"How?" Molly asked.

"Um," Danny shrugged his shoulders, turning to face Molly, "We hitchhike."

"Ok," Molly agreed, realizing that might be the only way.

CHAPTER 23

"Are you two coming with us?" Danny asked Luke and Ruth. Ruth and Luke glanced at each other.

"If it's all right with you, then, yeah we'll tag along," Luke said, stepping forward to shake Danny's hand.

"Ok. Where in California are we going?" Danny asked. Molly reached in her bag and pulled out the train tickets that Shelly had given her.

"It says here that we have to go to San Diego. That's where we'll find Mr. B. Red. He'll take us to Hawaii, Danny. Where in California are you guys going?" Molly asked Luke and Ruth.

"Well, The Runaway Cabin is in Pasadena, I believe," Luke mentioned.

"Ok, we need a map," Molly declared.

In the little town of Taos, there was a little shop. Danny, Molly, Luke, and Ruth trekked across the dirt road and opened the door into a store full of colorful trinkets. The four kids couldn't help but stand in awe and amazement at the many overwhelming colors and smells. A large but short lady came out of a back room.

"Welcome!" the lady exclaimed and threw her hands in the air sending her long jet black hair into all different directions.

"Hi, uh, we need a map," Danny mentioned to the lady. The

lady came up to Danny and gave him a big hug and then two kisses on each cheek. Danny squirmed and turned pink, but the lady just hugged him again. Then the lady came and hugged and kissed each kid.

After her big introduction, she folded her hands and then put them on her hips.

"Now, how can I help you?" the lady asked, smiling from ear to ear.

"Yeah, we need a map," Danny said once more.

"Right!" The lady's eyes lit up, "Follow me," she said and then turned and walked right back into the back room. Danny and Molly hesitated, but soon they all followed her.

Molly walked behind Danny with Luke and Ruth behind her. The back room was musty and dusty, much like the rest of the town, but it was cozy. It had three shelves over-flowing with fabric, candles, scents, jewelry, and many other interesting objects.

Molly followed Danny by turning left. Then they all stopped walking, and the lady bent down pulling up a brown box.

"Now, it might be dusty, but it still works," she said, taking off the lid. Then she pulled out a map. There were two maps. One of the United States and the other was one of the world. Molly could only wonder how people could fit the whole entire world on one small piece of paper. Again, Molly felt small.

"You can have them," the lady said, putting the lid back on the box, "I have extras," She smiled then set the box down. Then they all walked through the museum of colors and into the store room. The lady walked back around the counter.

"So, why do you need a map?" She asked, smiling. Molly wondered how one lady could possess so much joy.

"We're traveling. Do you know a place where we could

stay?" Danny asked her, peeking around. Molly remembered that it was four-thirty, and it would get dark in about an hour-and-a-half.

"Well, I mean there is the Taos Hotel," the lady paused. "But you don't want to stay there. Why don't you kids stay here for the night?" the lady asked.

"Uh, well we couldn't impose," Danny replied.

"No, no, it's fine," the lady smiled, "Please, I insist!"

"Well, I don't know. Um, my friends and I are going to go outside and talk. We'll let you know, thank you," Danny said, putting the maps in his back-pack and then he walked outside followed by Molly, Luke, and Ruth.

"Oh, and my name is Josephine, Josephine Monterary," She said, smiling and waving as Ruth closed the screen door. The four walked down the steps onto the dusty road into the hot blinding sun. They walked a couple feet away from the door and stood in a circle.

"Well, what do you think?" Danny asked the group. Ruth shrugged her shoulders.

"I am not too sure, but I believe that this Josephine is a kind lady," Luke said.

"Yeah, she is." Molly implied.

"Ruth?" Danny asked.

"Yeah, um, as long as she has some food and water, I'm good," Ruth replied.

"So, what? Are we going to stay with her?" Danny asked.

"Um, what if she's one of Ivan's men, or women?" Molly questioned.

"Molly's got a point," Danny noted.

"I don't know. I mean I guess anything's better than staying outside," Luke announced.

"So, do we have a plan?" Danny asked. Molly nodded her head along with Luke and Ruth. Josephine opened the screen door.

"So, have you made your plan?" she asked.

"Um, I believe so. I think we'll take you up on that offer. If you don't mind, then we'd like to stay with you?" Danny said.

"Why, yes, that's perfect!" You dears can sleep in the chairs in the storeroom. Uh, I'll go get them ready," Josephine said walking inside followed by Luke and Ruth.

CHAPTER 24

"So what do you think?" Danny asked Molly. Molly looked down at the sand that had gathered around her brown boots she had gotten from Madame Marine.

"I'm not sure Danny. I don't know about any of this," Molly blurted out.

"What do you mean?" Danny asked.

"Well," Molly bit at her lips, "I left the orphanage, hoping to get away from Ivan, forever. And it was all fine, then I met you and things just have gotten worse and worse," Molly looked at Danny.

"Whoa now, this isn't my fault," Danny said, taking a stand.

"I don't know Danny," Molly began.

"Look, I didn't even know of Ivan until just this morning," Danny replied, staring at Molly.

"Yeah, well," Molly was cut off by Danny.

"You're tired Molly. Go inside before you say something you'll regret," Danny insisted and pointed toward the screen door.

"You can't boss me around!" Molly yelled.

"I know that, but listen to yourself, Molly," Danny raised his voice. Molly glared at Danny while he glared back. Molly opened her mouth as if to say something, but the opening of the screen door cut her off.

"Hey you guys!" Ruth walked out unaware of the situation, "So, Josephine has some drinks ready." Molly and Danny both glared at Ruth.

"You know, I think I'll go in and wait inside," Ruth nodded her head and then slowly eased back inside and closed the door.

"Is there something that you'd like to say, Molly?" Danny asked, putting his hands in his jean pockets.

"Look," Molly took a breath, "This wasn't supposed to happen,"

"What?" Danny implied.

"Ivan. He ruins everything!" Molly threw her hands in the air.

"Hey, look, we got away from him. It was just a bump in the road, take a breath," Danny softly said.

"No, Danny. We didn't get away from him. He'll never stop hunting us. He'll never stop chasing us. Not until we're dead. You don't understand, Danny. Ivan is evil. He's got no heart," Molly's voice got quieter.

"Molly, you have to talk to me. What did he do that's so bad? Besides being a German spy and a mass murderer," Danny asked.

"He killed my parents," Molly looked at the ground.

"Hold up, you said that your mom left you and your dad got shot in a bank robbery,"

"I know, I lied," Molly looked up at Danny, who was in shock, "I didn't know if I could trust you." Danny didn't say anything, but his mouth still hung open.

"They knew Ivan, as a friend. I knew Ivan, as a friend. He was like an uncle. When I was eight, my parents found out that he was working with Germany to try and get another war started, so he killed them. He burned our house down. The authorities think that my parents died in a house fire and I survived, but what they don't know is that Ivan had already knocked them unconscious. He burned them alive. I was sent to an orphanage in Boston originally. Ivan still thinks that I am there. He doesn't recognize me, I think," Molly finished by looking around to see if anyone had overheard.

"I'm sorry," he eventually mustered out. Molly just nodded her head. "I didn't know."

"Well, now you do, and I would prefer it if you would keep this between us," Molly insisted to Danny. He nodded. Molly didn't know what was yet to come. She knew that somehow, sometime, they would have to get Ivan caught. He needed to go to prison, forever.

CHAPTER 25

"I guess we should go inside and eat with the others," Danny suggested. Molly just nodded her head.

"You go on in. I'll be there in a minute," Molly told him. Danny walked up the four creaky wood steps, opened the screen door, and walked inside, while the screen door slammed shut behind him.

Molly looked around at the town. She noticed a little restaurant. The police station, the Taos Hotel, a general store, and then Josephine's store. Molly saw few people in this little town. Most people were indoors and out of the heat. However, there were some who were out. On the porch of Taos Hotel were four rocking chairs. Two on each side of the somewhat large front deck.

In one of the chairs sat a gentleman. Molly couldn't see his eyes nor most of his face because his brown cowboy hat was blocking both. Underneath the shade of the hat Molly could see a mustache and a short beard. He wore brown pants, brown boots, a white shirt with a brown vest on top. Molly figured he was asleep in the rocking chair.

Then the man lifted his hand and moved his hat up. He was looking at Molly who just looked back. He must have sensed someone was watching him, Molly thought. Molly could tell a lot about someone by their eyes. The man had soft blue eyes which Molly noticed were full of courage and determination.

The man stood up and walked inside the Taos Hotel. Of the couple seconds that Molly saw him standing, she saw a big leather belt that had a pistol and a knife on it. She also noticed that he was no young man. Molly assumed he was probably in his late fifties or early sixties.

Molly had never told anyone of her secret. Recalling the thought of her parents made her want to cry. Of course, Danny knew that something else had happened to Molly because of Ivan, and it was only a matter of time before he would find out.

Molly remembered all of the times that she would play with Ivan in the backyard of their sweet cozy home. Ivan had been a life-long friend of Molly's dad. Molly remembered Ivan always being there as far back as she could think. The warm and pleasant memories were always the hardest for Molly to remember.

So much had happened since she knew Ivan as a friend. Since she was so young, most of the memories were fuzzy, all except the one when her house burned down. Molly remembered being asleep in her parents' bed. Molly had had a fever that day and the day before, so she mostly slept. She didn't know that Ivan had snuck into her house. Molly remembered waking up and walking down the hall.

She saw Ivan walk out the front door leaving her parents looking lifeless on the floor. Then she saw Ivan throw something into the house, and next, there were flames everywhere. Molly was so scared and she remembered not being able to breathe. So, she saw the front door wide open a couple feet away. She slowly crawled out and onto the front porch.

The rest of that day, and the next three, Molly couldn't remember. She vaguely remembered a month after that. Before she could even think, she was placed in an orphanage. For as long as she could remember, that's where she stayed. In an orphanage. It wasn't always the same orphanage, but it was an orphanage.

Molly could remember her parents talking to her three days before they were killed. They told her that there were good people and bad people in the world. That there would come a time when they wouldn't be around to help her through life and she would have to make her own choices. That when someone is in need of help you help them. Most importantly, when things went downhill, not to get frightened. They told her that things would most definitely go down hill, but you keep your head up and free of worry.

Molly had no clue why they told her these things. As far as she was concerned, her life was perfect. She was happy, content. But that changed in a blink of an eye. Molly was not prepared for it, but it came so quickly. She was alone. Alone to navigate her way through life and through the world. Obviously, life had not been very kind to Molly, but when has life ever been kind to anyone?

However, they told her these things because they knew of Ivan's secret. They suspected what was going to happen to them. They knew they had to tell someone. Sadly, they weren't quick enough. Molly vowed to be quick enough to get Ivan caught. At her last orphanage, Ivan came, and she overheard him speaking. She found out real quick who and what he was. And then she remembered him. He also found out that she knew. And the funny fact was that he didn't recognize her. Ever since then, he's been hunting her down.

Molly was completely aloof to the rest of the world. She stood in front of Josephine's store lost in her own thoughts. A loud noise and a cry brought her back to reality. She turned around to face the Taos Hotel.

In a blink of an eye, she saw the old man kick a young man off the front porch and onto the dirt road where dust and sand went flying. Molly's first instinct was to run over there and help the man who was kicked, but as she stood and watched more she realized that the man was a thief. The old man grabbed the young man by the collar and reached into the young man's jacket pockets and pulled out quite a lot of cash.

By now, most people were out watching the scene. The owner of the Taos Hotel, a short, thick man with what's left of little jet black hair and tiny spectacles, stood on the front porch of his hotel with his arms crossed and a stern expression on his face.

"Now get out of here," Molly heard the old man roar as he let go of the young man's collar. The young man then took off running. The old man walked up the motel steps and handed the owner the cash. They had a conversation, which Molly could not hear. She was too far away.

CHAPTER 26

"What was that?" Molly recognized Josephine's voice to her left. Molly turned in that direction to see Josephine, Luke, Ruth, and Danny, all gathered on the front porch of the store. They must have heard the cries.

"I'm not sure," Molly said confused.

"Are you ok?" Ruth came down the steps and asked Molly.

"Oh yeah, I'm fine," Molly replied. Then Josephine walked down the steps, holding her dress, which was far too long for her short body, and she strolled across the dirt road. The kids looked at each other and then took no hesitation in following her.

As they approached the Taos Hotel, the owner, and the old man on the front porch, Molly began to feel a little nervous.

Josephine walked fearlessly up the front steps and joined right into the conversation the old man and the owner were having.

"Hello, Miguel," She nodded toward the owner, "Harvey," She nodded toward the old man, "Would either of you like to explain what might've just happened?"

"Well, this freak of a human being just," Miguel began.

"What Miguel is saying, Miss Josephine, is that a man tried to rob his cash register. That's all, nothing important," Harvey said as he sat down in one of the rocking chairs. Harvey pulled out a big brown pipe and lit it and began to smoke it.

"Well, I'll be," Josephine said, putting her hand on her heart. Molly got a better look at the old man, Harvey. He had a gray mustache and short gray beard. He had wrinkles all over his tan face. Behind his mustache and beard, she could see a hint of bright red lips. His bright blue eyes sparkled making him look younger than he actually was.

The man glanced at Molly. He took his cowboy hat and tilted it. Showing a weak smile, he returned back into his own world and his brown pipe.

Molly turned around and noticed Josephine and Miguel in a deep conversation. Luke and Ruth sat on the steps of the hotel. Danny stood on the steps leaning on a pillar of wood that supported the upper roof of the hotel. Danny seemed to be in deep thought staring at the slowly setting sun.

Molly walked closer over to Josephine and Miguel.

"And that's what I said," Molly listened to Migeul say.

"And he took it anyway?" Josephine asked in shock, "Do you know who the man was?"

"Yup. No clue," Miguel replied, putting his hands on his hips.

"Did you get all of the money back?" Josephine asked intently.

"I believe so. Old Harvey here saved me, once more," Miguel motioned toward Harvey who hadn't moved from his position in the rocking chair.

"Well, what would we do without you, Harvey?" Josephine walked over to Havery and patted his arm.

"Aw, well thank you, but it was nothing to get worked up about," Harvey said.

"Of course," Josephine smiled and walked back over to Miguel.

"Why did he take the money?" Molly asked Miguel.

"Well, who might you be? Josephine, I didn't know you had kids?" Migeul asked, pointing to Molly, Danny, Luke, and Ruth.

"Oh heavens no. These four wandered up on my doorstep," Josephine clapped her chubby hands together, smiling.

"Oh, are you all traveling?" Miguel asked Molly.

"Yes sir, but why did that man take the money?" Molly asked once more.

"Only God knows, child. Where are you headed?" Miguel said, taking his spectacles off and cleaning them. He spit on each tiny round piece of clear glass and then wiped them with his white apron that hung just below his knees.

"Um, Arizona and then to California," Molly answered. She didn't like telling everyone where they were going in case of Ivan. And besides, she wasn't exactly lying.

"Aww, I see," Miguel said, nodding his head. Then Harvey stood up and began to open the hotel screen door.

"Oh, speak of the devil," Miguel laid a hand on Harvey's shoulder, "Harvey here just so happens to be headed to Polacca, Arizona. Isn't that right Harvey?"

"That's true Miguel, but I' don't need no comp-"

"Why don't you kids tag along with old Harvey? He'll take you safely into Arizona and get you kids on a train headed to California," Miguel smiled.

"Um, well, I think we should go alone Mr. Miguel, thank you thou-" Molly began.

"Nonsense, Harvey'll give you a ride in his wagon, won't you Harvey?" Miguel insisted. Harvey lifted his head and closed his eyes.

"Why not? We leave in the morning, sunrise. Oh and y'all better get inside. It'll be dark soon and cold," Harvey said, taking Miguel's hand off his shoulder and walking into the hotel.

"You'll have to excuse him. Well it's settled then," Miguel said, clapping his hands and rubbing them together, "Now, who'd like to come in and get a bite to eat? It's on me,"

"Oh, we couldn't impose, Miguel," Josephine said.

"Naw, you're invited," Miguel smiled.

"Uh well, kids?" Josephine turned to face the kids.

"Yeah, I think it's a great idea. What's for dinner?" Ruth asked.

"See, they all agree. It's the right choice, Josephine, come on," Miguel asked again.

"Well, all right. Let's go children," Josephine said as they stepped into the Taos Hotel for a big scrumptious dinner.

CHAPTER 27

Molly walked inside the hotel with Danny on her right and Luke and Ruth on her left. The light was rather dim inside, but there was an aroma of tantalizingly fresh food. She looked to her left and saw a staircase leading up to rooms, she guessed. To her right she noticed a counter. Behind the counter were shelves that had papers stacked inside each little compartment of wood.

In front of Molly, there was a big long wooden table. It had a red table cloth with golden designs. The table had wooden benches that were as long as the table, probably twelve feet long. The room that Molly stood in was very large. Molly guessed that if someone had a birthday party, or a wedding, this is where it was held. Molly surmised that it was the town-gathering place. There was a spirit in the room that would make any person lively and joyful.

"You're in luck children. Tonight is my son, Davy's, fourth birthday. We're celebrating him," Miguel said happily. Then a little figure ran up. He had brown eyes, brown hair, and tan skin.

"Papa," the little boy said as Miguel picked him up and gave him a hug.

"Davy, my son. Happy birthday," Miguel smiled. "Oh, you remember Miss Josephine. Yes, she's here to celebrate your birthday. And these are some of her friends," Miguel pointed to the kids. Davy looked shyly at the kids. When Miguel set him down, Davy ran off.

"We're going to eat in about thirty minutes. Please," Miguel clapped his hands together, "make yourselves at home," Miguel then walked off saying hello to people on his way over to a tall beautiful lady. Miguel gave her a kiss on the cheek before the couple stood and watched their little boy play games with his friends.

Molly, Danny, Luke, and Ruth all stood still for a couple moments. They had no clue what to do.

"Is that?" Ruth peered toward the food table, "Ahh, yes it is, corn!" Ruth ran over to the short small table that had little food covering it. Ruth began to dive into the yummy foods.

In the large hotel gathering room, the far left corner beside the doors was a little place which had books on shelves and two chairs. Luke took no hesitation in parading over, grabbing a stack of books, and sitting down in one of the chairs. Luke was lost in his own world.

Molly and Danny still stood waiting for something to do. There were quite a lot of people in the large room. The children all hung out in a corner playing. Most of the men sat around a table playing cards or shooting darts at a dart board that hung in the far right corner. The ladies sat around another table chit-chatting about, probably, gossip.

"I haven't played darts in a while," Danny shared. Molly looked over at him and noticed that he was staring right at the four big men playing darts.

"Then go play," Molly replied.

"No, they wouldn't let me," Danny said, second guessing himself.

"How would you know? Have you asked?" Molly asked.

"Well, no, but, I mean look at them. They're huge," Danny said.

"The darts aren't that big," Molly replied.

"I wasn't talking about the darts, Molly,"

"Oh. What were you talking-" Molly began, but Danny pointed.

"The men," Danny said as his face almost went pale. Molly began to laugh.

"They're just men, Danny," Molly stated.

"Yeah, I would look like a fool," Danny professed, trying to tear his blue eyes away from the darts. Molly glanced back and forth from the dartboard to Danny.

"Oh come on you big baby," Molly spoke as she grabbed Danny's arm and then began to drag him over towards the darts in the far right corner.

"Hey, what are you doing? Molly, stop it, no," Danny demanded the whole way there, but they eventually reached the darts and the big men.

"Excuse me fellows, my friend here," Molly pushed Danny forward, "was wondering if he could join your game of darts?" The men looked at each other and then began to howl.

"Well," Molly said after a few seconds and the men wouldn't quit laughing.

"Uh, sorry," one man said, drying a tear from his eye, "I mean, if he thinks he can handle it, then sure kid, come on." Handing Danny a dart, the boy stepped forward, took a breath, held his arm up, and then gently but forcefully released the dart. The dart hit the wall beside the board.

Once again, the men roared hysterically. Danny swallowed. Then, he walked up to the board, took the dart out of the wall, and with the men still laughing got himself ready to throw the dart yet another time. Danny pulled his arm up, steadied himself, focused and then he released it. The dart hit the very center of the board.

The men immediately silenced their laughter, and Danny

smiled. The men strutted closer to Danny. They gathered around him practically growling. Danny tensed up, but then the man right in front of Danny's face smiled a big toothy smile. They all then began to pat Danny on the back.

"You did good, boy. What's your name?" one man asked.

"Danny."

"Well, Danny, why don't you play a game of darts with the big boys?" Then all of the men once again began to whoop. Danny joined in the laugh. With Danny taken care of, Molly left and meandered around the large room. She glanced back frequently to make sure that Danny hadn't gotten trampled, but every time she did, he was quite fine.

Molly continued moving around the large cheerful room. The only thing that she saw was happiness. It had been a while since Molly felt this happy and safe. Of course, she was still on guard for Ivan and his men.

Molly shuffled over to the corner by the front doors. She plopped down in a wood chair that was somewhat comfortable. To her left, on the other side of the front doors, was Luke, who was completely lost in a book about health and science. Ruth was still picking and choosing her favorite foods from the little food table. Molly felt bad for the red haired twins. Even though they both seemed happy, Molly could only wonder how they felt on the inside.

CHAPTER 28

Molly's attention was brought away from the twins to an old man walking up the steps to the rooms. Molly saw the back of his brown cowboy hat and knew that it was Harvey. Just then, he turned around and looked at Molly. He stopped dead still on the stairs and stared into Molly's eyes.

However, as quickly as he stopped he was moving up the stairs once again and then he disappeared into another level of the wood floor. Molly still stared at the stairs though.

"He's a strange man, huh?" Miguel asked Molly to her right. Molly stood up.

"Who is he?" Molly asked Miguel who folded his arms across his chest.

"Harvey Jones," Migeul took a breath, "He showed up on my doorstep three months ago. He asked if he could work here. I said, 'No I'm good,' but he stayed around. He began to catch thieves and robbers in the town. He saved my boy once, from choking. So, now I pay him in food and a roof over his head. He doesn't speak much though," Miguel shared.

"Do you know where he's from?" Molly couldn't help but ask. Migeul shook his head.

"Like I said, he doesn't say much of anything," Miguel then smiled at Molly as he walked off. Molly's curious self began to wonder and imagine as she sat back down in the wood chair. Was he a criminal? An undercover sheriff? Or was he one of

Ivan's men?

"Hello," Molly looked up and saw Danny looking at her waving his hand. "I thought you were dead or something," Danny went over to one of the tables and grabbed a chair. He picked it up and brought it over to Molly and then set it down and sat in it. "You were in deep, deep thought. What were you thinking about?" Danny asked her.

"Harvey," Molly said, "Does he seem fishy to you?"

"He seems like someone I don't want to mess with," Danny laughed.

"That's true. Miguel said he showed up three months ago. That he's been catching thieves and stuff all around town. Miguel said that he doesn't say much," Molly finished.

"Ok, so what's your point? Enlighten me, Molly," Danny said with a big toothy smile.

"Do you even know what 'enlighten me' means?" Molly asked, joyfully laughing.

"Ah, well no, but I heard one of those ladies say it," Danny stuttered, looking at the gossip ladies.

"Oh, I see," Molly laughed once more, "I don't know Danny. He just seems, strange,"

"Do you think he's one of Ivan's men?" Danny seriously and quietly asked. Molly shook her head side to side.

"I don't know," Molly shrugged.

"Well, apparently we're supposed to ride to Polacca, Arizona with him," Danny said.

"Yeah, what if he is one of Ivan's men? He'll turn us in," Molly replied.

"Maybe, but we might have to take that chance," Danny said, folding his hands underneath his chin.

"I don't know Danny, the twins have been through a lot,"

Molly replied.

"Molly, the twins are fine. How bad do you want to get to Hawaii?" Danny asked her.

"More than anything," Molly closed her eyes and imagined the blue waters and white sand.

"Ok, well, we're going to have to make some hard decisions, this being one of them," Danny said, "If we don't go with Harvey......."

"Jones," Molly implied.

"Harvey Jones, then we are probably going to have to walk and that could take months," Danny finished.

"True, so, I guess we go with him," Molly said unsure.

"I think so, and besides if anything goes wrong, there'll be four of us and only one of him," Danny smiled. Molly smiled back, but she was still unsure of going with the strange old man who had little to say about anything.

CHAPTER 29

Molly still could not believe what they were doing. Where they were. What had happened. The thought that her journey to get to freedom was slowly failing, occurred quite numerously. She couldn't help but feel bad for bringing Danny along. For all she knew, they got captured and were going to be killed if it were not for Antonio who decided that what he was doing was wrong.

She had a lot to think about. The trials and possible dangers till ahead. Is freedom worth it? The list included: staying the night with Josephine, riding with Harvey Jones on to Arizona, getting on a train in Polacca Arizona, then going to California where Danny and she would part ways with the redhead twins, and finally taking a boat to Hawaii. What would she do when she got to Hawaii? Would she ever see Danny again? As much as she did not want to think about it, Danny had been a friend to her. He was nice to her, which was rare for Molly.

"Well, I guess I'll go play darts, some more," Danny said, interrupting Molly's thoughts. Molly glanced up at Danny who had both his eyebrows up.

"Oh, sorry, I was thinking," Molly said. Danny shook his head and walked off.

As Molly sat by the front doors, she could feel a cold breeze of air pass through the wood every once in a while. She got the chills just thinking about how cold it must be outside. She always heard stories of how the dessert was hot in the day and freezing at night. She knew that when they rode with Harvey to Arizona they would have to bring many layers for the night and few for the day.

Molly looked up and around the large colorful room. Joesphine sat talking with the ladies. Miguel sat on the floor in a corner playing with Davy. Luke still relaxed in a chair beside the small bookshelf reading a book. Danny played darts, having to move his curly brown hair behind his ears quite often. Ruth, however, was staring right at Molly. Molly was quite startled when she saw Ruth looking at her.

Then Ruth started laughing and walked over to Molly. On her way though she dropped a piece of some type of desert. Molly watched the piece of food covered in some type of icing roll down Ruth's orange and red dress. Ruth bent over and picked up the piece of food. She walked over and threw it in a trash can, or maybe some ladies purse, and then walked back over to Molly. Ruth finished shoving some food in her mouth and then plopped down in the chair next to Molly.

"Did I scare ya'? Ruth asked grinning ear to ear.

"Um, no," Molly said.

"Oh, ok," Ruth paused, biting her lower lip, "You know, Luke and I really appreciate what you and Danny are doing for us. You know, helping us,"

"It's no problem," Molly stated, smiling gently.

"It's, it's nice to know that there's others like us, you know?" Ruth said.

"Yeah, I know. We have to stick together," Molly finished.

"So, what happened to you?" Ruth asked, waiting for Molly.

"What do you mean?" Molly asked, looking at Ruth.

"How did you find out about Ivan?" Ruth asked.

"Oh, um, well I've known him for a while now," Molly

paused, feeling Ruth's curious stare, "How about you?"

"Oh, well, while Luke and I were on our way to the Runaway Cabin, we stopped at an orphanage. We have some friends there. They gave us some food and what not and let us stay a couple days. Ivan showed up. Luke and I were staying in the attic you see, and when we heard someone coming up the steps we hid. It was Ivan, he was dragging a man up the steps. He pulled him up by his collar and told him to stand up. Ivan was livid. The man did something and Ivan did not like it. Ivan blurted out everything in the man's face, including," Ruth's voice got quiet, "The secret. Luke and I heard everything. Ivan found out we knew at the orphanage, but luckily we were out of his sight when he set fire to the attic,"

"He set fire to the attic?" Molly asked.

"Yup,"

"Did anyone die?" Molly asked.

"No, they got out, but me and Luke just ran. We ran really fast," Ruth nodded her head.

"I'm surprised he set fire to the attic," Molly paused, "Actually, I take that back, I'm not surprised,"

"Yeah," Ruth said.

"So, are you and Danny related?" Ruth asked.

"No," Molly replied, a little taken back.

"Oh, are you guys good friends?" Ruth asked. Molly found out real quick how talk-a-tiv Ruth was.

"Uh, well, I mean," Molly stuttered.

"Oh, I see, you just met," Ruth said, scratching her head.

"Yeah, pretty much," Molly said.

"So, why are you going to Hawaii?" Ruth asked more questions.

"Um, to get away from Ivan," Molly said smiling.

"That's a good reason," Ruth said underneath her breath, "What about Danny?"

"He's gonna join the Navy," Molly said.

"When's your birthday?" Ruth asked.

"The eighteenth," Molly replied.

"So, in three days?"

"Yup. What about your birthday?" Molly asked.

"Mine and Luke's birthday is in February. February 27 to be precise," Ruth smiled. Molly smiled back. Ruth was quite a character.

"Look at that," Ruth gawked at the food table, "They put more corn out. If you'll excuse me," Ruth said as she got up and walked over to the food table.

Molly smiled. Now, she had nothing to do, except sit lonely in the corner. Or she could go play darts. The thought had entered her mind more than once. She decided that since she had nothing else to do, she would play.

Molly stood up, took a breath, and then walked over to the far right corner where Danny and four other men were playing darts. As she walked over, she second guessed herself. However, she kept moving her legs, which began to feel more like jelly and sausage rather than flesh and bone.

Before she knew it, she was standing between the men and the dart board, right in the line of fire.

"Um, Molly, could you move?" Danny asked.

"Uh, well, I, I would like to play, please," Molly stuttered. The four men looked at each other and began to laugh, surprise surprise. Danny looked at Molly with three darts in his hand. He raised his eyebrows and stood speechless.

"What are you doing?" Danny mouthed to Molly.

"Playing," Molly mouthed back, sticking out her arm

waiting for a dart.

Danny closed his eyes, looked down, and then gave her a dart. Molly smiled. The men were still laughing, practically crying. Molly placed herself beside Danny, who licked his lips. Molly threw the dart, which hit the board. She took another dart. This time it hit the metal rim and fell to the ground. Then she took one more dart. This time it hit right smack center on the board. Danny began to nod his head.

"You're not that bad," Danny said, studying the board.

"Oh, don't sound so surprised," Molly laughed.

CHAPTER 30

For the next fifteen minutes Molly and Danny rivaled in an intense game of darts. Originally they tied, but when they rematched, Danny won. The four big men stood watching. They seemed to enjoy watching the game.

Finishing up the game and a little boastful about his win, Danny asked, "Have you ever played darts before?"

"No," Molly shook her head, "but I would watch my dad play."

"Could everyone gather around, please, just gather," Molly and Danny heard Miguel's voice. They both looked and watched everyone gathering in the center of the room. Molly and Danny were at the back of the crowd so it was quite hard to see what was going on. A couple seconds later, Migeul stood up on a chair allowing Molly and Danny to see him easier.

"My wife and I," Miguel smiled at the lovely tall lady, "would just like to thank each and every one of you for coming here to help us celebrate Davy's birthday. We are truly grateful. And now, Evan, who owns the restaurant down the street, you all should try it, it's amazing, but anyway, he offered to make a cake for my son. So, if we could give a round of applause for the cake," Miguel pointed both hands to a door that led into a back room and out walked a man, Evan, holding a tray with a little circle shape covered in icing.

Davy smiled and ran up to Evan. Evan set the cake on a

table and had Davy sit in a special chair. Everyone sang happy birthday to Davy, and then Davy dug into his little piece of goodness. As Molly and Danny admired Davy's cake devouring skills, Luke and Ruth sauntered over and stood with them.

For the rest of the evening, the only thing that the kids knew was happiness and joy. They loved the little town. It was like one big family. However, all good things must come to an end. At eight thirty, Josephine rounded the kids up to go back to her little shop.

"Thank you so much Miguel," Josephine gave Miguel a hug, "for the food, everything," Most of the other people had already gone home. The energy had settled in the room, for there were now few people in the room.

As Josephine hugged Maria, Miguel's wife, Miguel stood with his hands on his hips looking at the kids.

"Thank you so much for everything," Molly said to Miguel.

"It was my pleasure darling. You lovely kids made this night fun," Miguel said smiling.

"It was very fun sir. I enjoyed myself immensely," Danny said. Molly looked at Danny wondering where he was getting all the big words. He must have been listening in on the gossip ladies conversations.

"Ah, well, thank you," Miguel looked at the ground and then looked up, "You know kids, it's a dangerous world out there. You be safe now,"

"Thanks," The words slipped out of Molly's mouth. Miguel leaned into Danny and Molly's faces.

"Don't trust anyone," Miguel piped in a deep voice Molly didn't know he had and then Miguel leaned back out. Molly squinted her eyes and looked deep into Miguel's eyes. He knew something. About Ivan. He had known the whole time.

"all right dearies," Josephine turned around, interrupting

the silent conversation that Molly, Danny, and Miguel were having, "Are we ready?" Danny slowly nodded his head.

"Good, let's go then," Josephine said as she spun her head around whipping her jet black hair around also. She walked towards the two big front doors and opened them. Luke and Ruth followed Josephine. Luke with a stack of books, and Ruth with a stack of corn. Danny slowly walked past Miguel following Josephine, Luke and Ruth toward the front doors. When Josephine opened one of the doors, a cold chill whistled through the room.

"My goodness it is freezing," Josephine said as she took out a scarf and wraped it around her head and shoulders. She then continued out the door leaving Molly still staring at Miguel.

"At the train station in Polacca, you will find him. Beware, Molly Grace, he will try to kill you," Miguel whispered. Molly felt her fists tightened and as she licked her lips.

"Now, leave my child," Miguel said. Molly slowly moved her legs toward the front door where Danny stood waiting for her. His face was covered in questions. As Molly walked out of the door and into the freezing dark of night, she couldn't feel the cold. She was already too numb. How did Miguel know so much? She couldn't even think.

When she turned around and stared into the hotel, the smile that Miguel gave her, gave her courage to carry on. She knew she would see Ivan at the train station and he would see her. He would try to kill her, but she wouldn't let him. At least that's what Molly hoped.

CHAPTER 31

"Come now kids, hurry and get inside; it's quite cold out," Josphine said hurrying everyone up the wood steps to her little shop, "Got to close the door." Molly heard the screen door slam shut behind her and as the last little bit of light from the outside disappeared, she knew that Josephine had closed the big door also. It was pitch black and the only thing Molly could hear was the sound of breathing and Ruth eating corn.

Then a little spark and a flicker of light arose. Josephine took the match and lit a candle nearby, illuminating a little section of the store room. Then she went from candle to candle slowly lighting up the room. Soon the room was all lit up and the colors that filled the little space were ever so bright.

The reds from the scarves, the greens from the candles, the blue from the blankets, the pink from the dresses, the purple from the shoes, and the yellow from the little bouquet of flowers all overwhelmed Molly. Every time she walked into this little room it was like walking into a rainbow, Molly thought.

"Now then," Josephine put her hands on her hips, "We must get you dears settled for it is late because you all have a big day tomorrow." Josephine gathered blankets and pillows and eventually on the floor were two places to sleep and there were also two pairs of chairs that had been pushed together to make a concoction resembling a bench. Then she walked back into the back room.

Danny climbed into one of the chairs on the left side of the front door. Molly decided to get in the other chair on the right side of the front door. Ruth and Luke then got comfy with Ruth near the wall on the right side and Luke near the wall on the left. In the middle was a little walkway.

Since there were shelves up against the walls, Ruth and Luke had to be careful. As each child experienced comfort, the energy and excitement slowly faded as the only thing in the room was a bunch of tired kids. Josephine came back out from the back store room with her jet black hair in a long braid that was brought to the side.

"Now, I will be right back there," Josephine pointed to the back store room, "If you need me, I'm so glad I could help you darlings out a bit. Well, have a good night,"

"You too," Ruth said.

"Thank you again," Molly added.

"We really appreciate it," Danny mentioned. Luke simply nodded his head. Josephine just smiled, and then she closed the door. It was silent in the dark room. Even though a candle stayed lit in the far corner, Molly couldn't really see anyone's faces. She could make out who they were, but just couldn't see their expressions really well.

"Well, goodnight everyone," Ruth said, breaking the silence.

"Goodnight," Danny, Luke, and Molly all said at the same time. As Molly slowly fell asleep, her brain began to hurt from all of the thinking she was doing. Miguel knew of Ivan. He also said that she would see Ivan in Polacca. So many scenarios played in her head.

Exhaustion overwhelmed her for it had been a very long day. A very long past couple of days, actually. Molly had trouble remembering the last time she got a good night's sleep. As the thoughts in Molly's head slowly began to fade away, the only thing she felt was a calming sense of rest and relaxation; otherwise known as sleep.

"Molly," the voice was so far away it was barely hearable. "Molly," there it was again. "Molly, wake up!" Molly slowly stirred awake and opened her eyes to see nothing but darkness. She rearranged herself in her chair to get comfy.

"Molly, you awake?" Danny's voice whispered, but it was so loud to Molly's ears.

"No, I'm not awake," Molly said, trying to adjust her eyes to the darkness. The little candle was still lit in the far corner and Molly could see Ruth and Luke asleep like rocks.

"Ok, I need to talk to you," Danny said. Molly didn't say anything as she felt herself falling back asleep.

"Molly," the voice was stronger and a little louder this time and so Molly opened her eyes once more.

"What Danny? It's too late," Molly said.

"What did Miguel tell you?" Danny asked.

"What, Miguel didn't tell me any-" Molly stopped herself remembering what Miguel told her. "Wait, oh he said that Ivan would try to kill us in Polacca at the train station," Molly mumbled slowly, closing her eyes once more.

"How does Miguel know that? How does Muigel know about Ivan? Do we listen to him?" With each question that flooded out of Danny's mouth, Molly had no choice but to slowly wake up.

"I don't know, Danny," Molly sat up in the chair letting her legs hang down, "I don't know anything yet. Okay, for all I care Miguel somehow heard about Ivan and now he's just warning me to be careful. Or he doesn't even know about it and was just being funny. Yeah, he might not have even been talking about Ivan,"

"Now you're just guessing," Danny said sarcastically.

"Well, what else do you want me to do?" Molly asked, getting a little annoyed.

"I want you to talk to Miguel tomorrow and find out what he meant," Danny said. Molly didn't answer.

"Hello, don't tell me you fell back asleep," Danny said.

"No, I'm here. I just, well, I guess I'll do that," Molly breathed.

"Do you not want to?" Danny asked.

"No no, it's fine. I'll ask him," Molly replied.

"Okay, well, you can go back to sleep now, good night," Danny said.

"Goodnight, Danny," Molly replied as she curled back up in the chair. She slowly let her eyes get heavy and eventually close. As Molly slept, Danny thought. He was deep in thought about Ivan and Miguel and many other things. There were so many things to think about that he couldn't go to sleep. However, before he knew it, his eyes were shut and he was also in a much needed deep sleep.

CHAPTER 32

The next morning came quicker than Molly wanted. It seemed as though she only got one hour of sleep. It took so much strength for her to get out of the chair and to put her feet onto the cold wood floor. It was still dark out. The sun had not yet risen. Since Harvey Jones wanted to leave at sunrise, the kids had to be up before then to pack their things and prepare.

"Good morning everyone," Josephine's voice carried throughout the room. She was already dressed in a long pink and purple dress that was once again too long for her short body.

"I'll have some toast ready in a few minutes. You better get up, Harvey is already setting up the wagon," Josephine floated back to the back room.

Molly threw both arms in the air as she stretched her hands toward the roof. She let out a sigh that woke everyone up. After a few minutes, each child was awake and waiting for the toast. They had already packed up the blankets and pillows and set them neatly in a corner. Then they got all of their backpacks ready.Well, only Danny and Molly had backpacks.

"Here we are," Josephine eventually came from the back room with a plate of bread, butter, and jams. She set the plate on the counter. Molly could feel her mouth watering. Each kid got some toast and butter. For the first five minutes, it was silent as food was shoved into mouths.

"You kids, be safe now. It's a long way to Arizona,"

Josephine said. Since everyone's mouths were full they just nodded, "It's been my pleasure to care for you dears,"

"Thank you," Molly asserted when she swallowed her toast. Josephine just grinned. Eventually the sun began to peep out in the sky, so the kids knew it was time to go.

"Now, I noticed that you dears had packs," Josephine said pointing towards Molly and Danny, "But you dears did not. So, I packed a couple bags for you all," Josephine remarked as she gave Luke and Ruth each a back-pack. Inside there were five sandwiches in each bag, a blanket/jacket, some water canteens, and other little valuables.

"Thank you so much!" Luke exclaimed to Josephine. Molly and Danny smiled as they packed up their bags.

"You have been a blessing Miss Josephine," Ruth declared as she gave Josephine a hug.

"Oh, come now Josephine, get yourself together," Josephine mumbled to herself as she wiped away a tear.

Then they heard a knock at the door. Harvey's famous mustache and short gray beard showed up. As the sun began to wake up, the kids walked down the wood steps and onto the sandy dirt road. It was quiet in the early morning as the only thing that made sounds were the two horses hooked to the wagon and the kids setting their bags down in the wagon.

The wagon was, of course, made of wood, it had four, big, wooden wheels, a big bed, and between and behind the horses, sat a bench where Harvey would sit.

"Come on now, we have to get goin'. It's a long way to Polacca from here," Harvey said as he climbed up onto the bench. It swayed and shrunk as Harvey sat on top of it.

"Wait, wait," A voice came from the hotel and out ran Miguel, "Wait, I made these for you to take along," Miguel said as he handed Harvey two brown paper bags. Harvey nodded his head and set the brown paper bags down beside him.

"And goodbye to you dears," Miguel said as he helped Luke and Ruth climb in the back of the wagon. They both got comfy and then Miguel turned to Danny and Molly.

"And goodbye to you two," Miguel's expression changed from happy to serious.

"What did you mean?" Molly tried to ask.

"Shush child, come along now," Miguel said as he helped Molly in the wagon. Danny climbed up by himself and sat down beside Molly who was on her knees. Miguel closed the wooden board that acted as a gate on the back of the wagon.

Molly sat with her hands on the wood gate. Danny was beside her. It was only Josephine and Miguel who stood on the dirt road waving them off. Even though Harvey hadn't started moving the wagon yet, Molly already knew that something great and wonderful was once again slipping away through her fingers. The thing about hope ...

Molly looked at Josephine who was wiping a tear away from her chubby face. Molly took one last look at the short round lady, her jet black hair, her dress that was far too long, and her eyes that were an endless sea of love and comfort. And then Molly looked at Miguel. His apron that was stained, his glasses that were too small for his head, and his eyes that were filled with love, but also a mysterious shady past that Molly had no clue about.

It was silent until Harvey slapped the reins and a funny sound escaped his lips. The wagon jerked and Molly watched as Josephine and Miguel got smaller. Molly felt helpless as Miguel got farther and farther away. She knew she should've asked him what he meant. As the little town began to get smaller, the big world that surrounded Molly, began to get bigger. Even though she could barely make out Migeul and Josephine's figures, she didn't take her eyes off them.

"Molly," Miguel's voice called from a far distance, "Molly,

Klide Din, Klide Din," Since he was so far away, his voice faded, and Molly was left with a name that meant nothing for all she cared.

Even though the words "Klide Din" meant nothing to Molly, they left an imprint on her brain. She knew they meant something but what? Or who?

CHAPTER 33

Molly turned around and leaned against the back wooden board and stretched out her legs. Danny did the same. Ruth and Luke sat across from Molly and Danny with the same confused expression on their little freckled faces.

"What does Klide Din mean?" Ruth asked.

"I have no idea," Molly replied as Danny shrugged his shoulders.

"It sounds like a name, perhaps," Luke suggested.

"That's what I'm thinking," Danny implied.

"Well, here goes our long journey," Ruth said. They followed a dirt road. The simple little dirt road led straight to Polacca. They would find the train station in Polacca that would take them to California.

It had been a while since they left the little town of Taos and the sun was ever so hot. Ruth sat with one of Luke's books over her head to try to cover the sun from reaching her face. Luke leaned up right behind Harvey and therefore got some shade from Harvey. Danny and Molly shared an umbrella that Josephine had given them at the last minute.

Molly could feel her face was sunburned and red. Ruth and Luke had already been burned badly. Their pale skin was now red and pink. Danny however, only got darker. His skin was already tan, but it was only getting darker underneath the sun.

"We're making good time kids," Harvey said at noon when he pulled onto the reins and put the stick down that made sure the horses or the wagon couldn't move. The terrain around them hadn't changed much. It was all still dessert. There were a couple of cacti here and there but mostly just sand and more sand.

The kids watched as Harvey gave the horses some water and then as he took off his hat poured some water on his head and then drank some. Then he climbed back on the bench.

"All right, listen, I'm going to eat my lunch, but I can't eat and drive, so who wants to drive?" Harvey said plainly. None of the kids answered.

"You," Harvey pointed to Danny. Danny swallowed and then he stood up in the wagon bed, walked and climbed over Luke and then sat down on the right side of Harvey. Then Harvey dropped the reins in Danny's lap.

Molly had gotten closer to Ruth and Luke so as to see Danny drive.

"Don't crash boy," Harvey said sternly and then took a brown paper bag and pulled out a sandwich and then took a big bite of it. Danny finally slapped the reins and let out a squeaky sound, but the horses moved.

"Now listen, you gott'a giv em' a littl' oomf," Harvey said with his mouth full. He took one rein out of Danny's left shaky hand and slapped it hard on the horses behind. The horses then picked up speed. Danny sat straighter, but more tense.

As Harvey chewed his sandwich, Danny gently steered the reins. The horses weren't listening to Danny and then walked off the dirt road. Luckily the horses were going slow once again.

Harvey rolled his eyes and set his sandwich down. He took the reins from Danny's hands and steered the horses and wagon back onto the dirt road. And then Havey pulled the reins and stopped the horses.

"Look, you have to be stern or the horses won't listen

to you. Don't be afraid to slap 'em'. Also, these reins are like a mind translator, okay? When you're scared the horses can feel it through the reins, when you're mad they can feel it, if you don't care, they can feel it. Got it?" Harvey asked, and told, Danny by raising his eyebrows up.

"Yes sir," Danny swallowed. Then, Harvey gave the reins back to Danny. Danny slapped the horses and the wagon jerked forward so much to where Harvey grabbed the back of the bench to hold on, but after that Danny commanded the horses at a smooth pace.

CHAPTER 34

It had been at least an hour since Danny began to drive the wagon. Harvey sat silently beside Danny. He never said anything. Molly, Ruth, and Luke all sat around in the bed of the wagon.

Since it was the afternoon, the sun was ever so hot. Molly had never been so miserable before. The sun beat down hard on everyone's skin.

Thankfully, Harvey knew what he was doing. Molly knew little of the old man. He was quiet and only spoke when he needed to speak. There was something about him though, that made Molly and the other kids respect him. He spoke with authority and wisdom. Though he was quite old, Molly knew he would win any fight.

"You know, I don't think I like the desert," Ruth said. Molly looked at the young girl whose skin was the color of a lobster.

"Well, it's not exactly a pleasant walk in the park, that's for sure," Luke said, who was also a lobster.

"Yeah" Molly said and couldn't help but laugh a bit.

"So, when we get to Polacca, we have to find a train station right?" Ruth asked.

"I have to go to the train station to get some boxes and take them back to Arizona. So, you'll be right at the train station when we get there," Harvey said. Molly had thought he was asleep.

"Oh, will we have to jump on, or do we get seats?" Ruth asked.

"I'm not sure yet," Harvey said, taking his brown hat off his head and setting it on his face and he folded his hands behind his head.

Molly let herself slip away from the rest of the world. She went into deep thought. So much had happened. She had made some good friends, including Danny. She felt as though she had known Danny for a long time, but in reality, she had only known him for six days.

However, Molly was one who didn't like reality. Reality had been cruel and unfair to Molly. But then again, when has reality ever been fair to anyone?

Molly reached over towards her backpack, which was hot to the touch, and she opened the top. Inside, there was a canteen, a change of clothes, extra socks, some food, a pen, but of course, no journal. Molly still had no idea what had become of her precious gift, the journal. Luckily she only wrote about two pages worth. So, whoever had found it, probably Ivan, would not know much of where Molly was headed.

Molly had never been in the desert before this immense undertaking. She had never been out of New York City for that matter. She saw pictures and heard stories but had never experienced the adventures of the blazing hot neverending oceans. Molly spent most of her time when she was living at the orphanage, not at the orphanage. She would wander the alleyways and back streets of New York City.

The orphanage was, at most, a building. Molly was extremely thankful to have a roof over her head and three meals provided for her each day, but she would never say that she loved the orphanage. There was so much sorrow there.

The lady who owned the orphanage for girls, Miss D. was

a kind lady. She was ever so sweet, until she wasn't. If you forgot to do your chores, you were sent to bed with no supper. And for Molly, that happened quite often. Molly would get so distracted and curious, yet she could not help but explore the great city and would forget to return to the orphanage.

Molly was so thrilled to finally be away from the orphanage and the city. She never realized how much she would enjoy the country. Molly pulled her legs closer towards her to try to keep them underneath the shade of the wimpy excuse for an umbrella. Her arms were already both painfully sunburned, and she couldn't even imagine what her face looked like.

Thinking about how hot it was made her thirsty, so Molly reached into her back-pack and drank some water from the canteen. So far the scenery hadn't changed much at all. The heat from the sun made the dirt road ahead look like water. For miles to the left, it was just desert. And for miles toward the right, it was just desert.

CHAPTER 35

Danny drove the wagon pretty well. *Of course, he really only had to go straight, Molly giggled in her mind.* Molly recalled how when she first met Danny, six days ago, he was very immature and foolish. He was always lying and stealing. Molly wondered what had changed him. For now, he acted older than he was and as far as Molly knew, he hadn't lied or stolen anything.

Molly realized the reason she thought about Danny so much was because he knew her secret and about everything and still stuck with her. Danny was the only person in the whole wide world who actually knew Molly. And even though Molly trusted Danny, more than anyone, basically, she couldn't help but feel a little anxiety wondering if he would ever tell anyone her secrets.

Molly had a lot of thinking to do. Especially about Klide Din. She wondered if it was a place, or a name. However, she knew she would find out at the train station. Only Danny and she knew of the fact that something might happen at the train station.

Molly wondered if Harvey Jones knew of Ivan. Miguel knew of Ivan. It seemed as though Miguel was the only one who knew of Ivan in Taos, but how? Miguel must have had an encounter with Ivan sometime. Of course, Molly couldn't blame Miguel for not doing anything about it. Perhaps Ivan was threatening Miguel? Or, Miguel was just trying to keep his town, his wife, and his child safe from the evil Ivan.

The sound of crumpling paper being unwrapped captured Molly's attention. She peeked up and noticed Ruth was opening some paper and inside was a sandwich. She took a big bite, and of course, a smile arose across her face. Watching Ruth eat, Molly's stomach growled with anticipation. She grabbed a sandwich from her bag and began to eat. Eating allowed Molly's mind to ease for a moment, well at least switch topics.

Luke was falling asleep. She felt bad for the twins. Their skin was so pale, it just burned. They appeared Irish to Molly. Molly didn't really know what she was. Molly thought she remembered her parents telling her that her mother's parents were American Indian. That's what Molly's mom was, mostly American Indian. And Molly wasn't quite sure of her father. So, when people asked Molly about her heritage, she would just say American Indian or that she did not know.

Danny looked, well she wasn't really sure. He was born in Tennessee, and his mother was quite country, he had said before. But Danny also had some type of tropical jean in him. Maybe his father was from some tropical island? Molly didn't know.

Of course Harvey Jones, as well as Harvey's parents, were probably rocks. The old man had hardly any emotion. With his toughness, Molly figured his parents were also. Molly could tell that Harvey had gone through quite some winters. He was also experienced in all scenarios, or so she thought.

Molly finished the last bite of her sandwich, and she regretted eating it so fast. She wished she had more, but oh well. Sleeping after a meal was a perfect idea. Just a quick cat nap, she told herself.

Molly jolted awake. The wagon had stopped, making everyone jerk. Molly could feel her heart jumping out of her chest as she tried to calm herself from the startling awakening.

"All right, we'll have to make camp here for tonight," Harvey declared as he jumped down from the seat of the wagon, "I've got to fix this wheel." Harvey glared at Danny. Danny made a somewhat terrified grin as he slowly climbed off the bench. Danny unhooked the horses from all their equipment.

Molly stood up in the bed of the wagon and reached her arms toward the sky. The wagon was stopped a little to the left of the dirt road, out of the way. It was a tiny clearing where they could easily stay the frigid night.

"What did I miss?" Molly asked knowing that she missed something.

"Well," Ruth stood up, "you fell asleep and we rode. And rode some more. And rode some more. And rode some more. And rode some-"

"Get on with it Ruth," Luke pushed as he stood up in the bed of the wagon.

"I'm working on it. Chill out. Anyway, we rode for a long time through the hot sun with no change of scenery. And then about five minutes ago, Danny was driving right, like he has been doing the past six hours, and he sneezed really big and somehow managed to jerk the horses, and so the back end of the wagon went off the road and hit a rock. It messed up the wheel. I don't know how you didn't wake up," Ruth laughed as she jumped out of the wagon bed followed by Luke.

"Me neither," Molly wondered aloud, climbing out of the wagon bed. When her feet hit the ground, dust went into the air. The ground was hard, even though it looked as if it would be soft.

Molly went over to Danny who was still trying to help the horses. Ruth and Luke went over and watched Harvey trying to fix the back left wheel.

"So," Molly began, "you went off the road, huh?"

"Yeah," Danny paused, "It was an accident,"

"You could have killed me," Molly said plainly.

"Aw, don't even start. You were snoozen. You didn't even know what was going on," Danny joked.

"Fair enough," Molly said, "What are the horses' names?"

"So, this one is Apple Pie," Danny said, touching the one in front of him by stroking the matted maine of brown hair, "and that one is Carmel," Danny said pointing to the horse on the left side of the wagon.

"Which is your favorite?" Molly asked as she slowly reached her hand out to touch Apple Pie.

Danny looked at Molly, "Do not ask such a question," Danny whispered. "You may hurt their feelings,"

Molly chuckled. Ruth and Luke walked around the wagon to meet Danny and Molly.

"Harvey told us," Luke pointed to Ruth and himself, "to go get some twigs or something to start a fire."

Then Luke and Ruth scuttled off and tracked, not far off, for some twigs or sticks. Molly reached over the side of the wagon and pulled out her back-pack. Then she walked a couple feet from the wagon and set it down. Molly plopped on the sandy hard ground.

The sandy ground that Molly sat on was actually quite cool. As Molly explored her surroundings with her eyes, the sun was beginning to set. Molly remembered falling asleep around one, and the sun was now setting. Wow, she must have slept for a long time.

It was most likely around six. Harvey was still fixing the wheel, and he would probably be at it for a while. Danny was trying to tie up the horses to the wagon and then find a big rock to put underneath a wagon wheel so as to keep it from going anywhere. Ruth and Luke were still looking around for twigs. Luke had some wood looking pieces in his hands and Ruth had, well nothing yet.

Molly sat on the ground and watched the sunset. *The sun was so much bigger in the desert she thought.* Almost as if she and the sun were face to face. In the city, she could see the sunset, but it wasn't as magical as it was here she thought. Molly could almost feel the last little bit of warmth coming from the slowly setting sun.The temperature had dropped drastically. The frigid air consumed her hot sun-burned skin.

CHAPTER 36

It had taken a while to get the little fire started, but eventually there were little flames producing a somewhat small amount of heat. It was completely dark now and the temperature had dropped a lot.

Molly had eaten a sandwich for dinner and so did Danny and the others. Silence filled the air as they gathered around the little fire. Luke and Ruth huddled close together to try to keep themselves warmer. Danny had on a flannel and then a jacket on top of that so he appeared quite comfortable.

Harvey Jones was not moved by the freezing chill that filled the air. He didn't seem to mind it at all. Apple Pie and Caramel both laid on the hard ground still tied up to the wagon.

The cold didn't really bother Molly much. She was absorbed in her own thoughts, which was normal. She wondered what the future held, but she was ready, or so she hoped.

Molly wondered about Ivan. She didn't grasp how the tall man had not yet recognized her. Of course she was only eight when he last saw her. She had grown a little taller and her hair was longer, but still she didn't understand. Molly knew little of Ivan's past.

It had been so long since she was close to him, and yet even when she was close to him, he hardly said anything about himself. Molly wondered how long his scheme had been going on before her parents discovered it. Just a couple days after her parents found out about Ivan, they were murdered by Ivan.

Molly thought, well, she knew that her parents were Ivan's first victims. Molly didn't know of everyone that he had killed, but she shamefully knew it was a larger number than just two.

"We'll have to hit the hay soon," Harvey said, "We have to wake up early and get movin'." Danny nodded his head along with the others.

"Well, goodnight then," Ruth said as she stood up. She walked over to the wagon and climbed inside making herself a cozy little place to sleep. Soon after, Luke went and slept in the wagon also.

Molly hadn't moved. She was in deep thought, and also partly because her feet were frozen. The time seemed to be flying by. Molly sat leaning on a large rock and she was actually quite comfy, using her jacket as a blanket. Harvey sat leaning with his back on one of the wagon tires. Danny sat leaning on a log.

It was getting late, but Molly and Danny were still sitting wide awake. Harvey was nowhere near sleep. He sat with his pipe in his mouth staring into the fire. Danny's eyelids slowly began to get heavier.

"Well, I think I'll go to sleep now," Danny said as he scooted down and stretched out to where the log was acting as a pillow for his head. He then took off his jacket and covered himself with it, like it was a blanket.

After twenty minutes, Danny was out. Luke and Ruth had long been asleep in the bed of the wagon.

"You know, you should go to sleep while you can," Harvey said.

"Well, what about you?" Molly asked.

"I'm old, sleep isn't as important for me as it is for you," Harvey said.

"I might be young, but I know enough to know that is not true," Molly snickered. Harvey just raised his eyebrows.

"Besides, I'm keeping watch," Harvey said.

"What makes you think I can't keep watch?" Molly asked.

"Look little girl," Harvey looked up and said, "I don't know who you are, or who you think you are, but...," Harvey paused, "You are strange; I'll tell you that."

Then it was quiet as silence filled the air.

"Why are you so tough?" Molly asked out of the blue. Harvey slowly looked up and let out a little laugh. Then he looked back down at the fire. A few minutes passed.

"So, you're just going to ignore me?" Molly asked.

"Did your parents not teach you any manners?" Harvey asked.

"No, they died before they could really teach me anything," Molly replied.

"Huh, sorry, kid," Harvey grunted, "Happens to the best of us."

"So, what's your story?" Molly asked. Harvey looked up.

"You just don't quit do you?" Harvey said. Molly was silent waiting for Harvey to tell his story.

"I was born on April 20, a long time ago. I grew up with my dad, mom, three brothers, and two sisters," Harvey finished.

"That's it!?" Molly asked. Harvey took the pipe out of his mouth.

"No friends? No fights? No wife? No kids? No nothing?" Molly appealed dramatically.

"I had a wife once," Harvey said quietly, "and a son."

"What happened to them?" Molly asked. Harvey paused, then looked up.

"It's time for you to get some sleep," Harvey said as he stood and walked behind the wagon. Molly tried to get comfortable leaning on the large rock. If she had her journal, this is when she would write in it, but as hope goes in her life, she didn't have it.

She soon closed her eyes and entered into a world, her imagination, that was much better than the real world. A world that was safe. A world with no villains. A world where people were good. A world where Ivan didn't exist. A world that wasn't real.

CHAPTER 37

The abrupt sound of Harvey packing up camp woke up Molly. The sun had not yet risen and therefore, it was still very early. Luke and Ruth were both already up. It appeared as though Danny had just woken up, like Molly.

As Molly slowly stood up, allowing her jacket, her blanket, to fall to the ground, she could feel the cold air as it bit at her face. Molly's feet were frozen icicles and her hands and fingers were blue.

Molly began to pack up her things, which wasn't much. She noticed that the twins were still pink lobsters. Danny was ever so tan, but his nose was red from the cold making him look like a clown.

Molly could only imagine what she looked like, but honestly, she didn't care. She was too focused on getting to Polacca, Arizona. They would be arriving there sometime late tonight. Molly had a lot to think about. Of course, it seemed as though that's all she did, but she had to figure out who or what Klide Din was. The words that Miguel yelled to Molly as she left Taos.

And Ivan. Ivan Gualy. The evil human that probably wasn't even human. He was a monster, killing those who threatened him. Such as Molly's parents. Molly knew that Ivan needed to go. But she didn't know how or when.

So far no one had said a word. Molly figured it was

still too early and therefore, not everyone was awake. However, Molly was used to waking up before the sun. At the orphanage, Molly did that every morning. Harvey was awake though. Molly wondered if he even went to sleep.

Before she knew it, they were all once again piled in the big wagon bed, with Harvey Jones and Danny on the front board. Apple Pie and Carmel were both hooked up and ready to go for another day. Danny slapped the reins and they were off, headed to Polacca.

Molly looked back at the camp to make sure they hadn't forgotten anything. The only thing that was left was a little steam from where the fire once was. Ruth looked as though she was still asleep. Luke was trying to read a book on the sky that Josephine had given him, but it was just too dark.

The wagon jerked and so did Molly. It was bright out and the sun was ever so hot. However, the scenery had not changed. Molly realized that she had fallen asleep and the hours ticked by. It was now nine in the morning. She had slept around four hours from when they started.

Harvey put the break on and climbed out. He banged on the side of the wooden wagon awaking Ruth and Luke who had also fallen asleep. Danny had been driving.

"Water break," Harvey said. The wagon had stopped beside a little creek. Well, it was hardly that, but close enough to where there was fresh drinkable water. The horses were able to bend down and drink the water the way the wagon was stopped. Harvey Jones filled up his canteen and on one knee he drank the water.

The kids did the same. Danny climbed out of the wagon and knelt beside Molly to fill up his canteen. Molly looked at him and almost spat her water out. The boy looked terrible.

He had dark circles underneath his eyes. His lips were chapped. His eyes were also red from rubbing. His cheeks were bright red. He was sweating buckets. And worst of all, his hair was a matted awful mess.

"Well, I'll be George's uncle. You look awful, Danny," Molly said as she couldn't stop staring at his face.

"Thanks. I feel great," Danny said in a cracky harsh voice as he swayed about to fall over.

"No, I don't think you do," Molly said. Danny tried to smile but his eyes began fluttering and then they shut completely and Danny fell sideways onto the hard sand, still as the stone beside him.

"Danny!" Molly said as she jumped and ran over to him.

"Danny, wake up!" Molly began to shake him. Harvey Jones, Ruth and Luke all came running over.

"Out of the way," Harvey said as he knelt down beside Danny's face. Harvey rolled Danny over onto his back. Then he took his canteen, opened the lid and poured the water on Danny's face. Danny began to cough as he tried to sit up.

"Stay down boy," Harvey demanded, "I see you're pretty exhausted. Heat exhaustion I believe," Harvey took a breath and sat back. Molly looked at Harvey and then at Danny.

"Is he gonna be all right?" Molly asked Harvey.

"Yeah, he'll be fine in a day and after some rest and water," Harvey replied. Danny then sat up with his head and body still swaying from the dizziness. Harvey kept his hand on Danny's back to keep him steady.

"Come on kid, let's get you some water," Harvey said, handing Danny's canteen to Molly to fill it up. Molly walked over the little tiny creek and filled up Danny's canteen. Then she walked back and handed it to Danny.

"Watch him," Harvey said standing up going to check on the horses.

"How do you feel?" Molly asked as Danny drank the water.

"Fine," Danny swallowed.

"Do you want more water?" Molly asked.

"I will in a minute, but I can get it," Danny replied, looking at the ground.

"I guess I'll drive," Harvey said as he walked back over.

"That was awfully scary," Ruth said.

"I thought you were dead," Luke implied. Danny let out a little laugh.

"Well, we better get a move on if we want to get to Polacca tonight," Harvey said.

Everyone stood up and finished drinking their water, though Danny was a little slow. Harvey helped Danny get in the wagon bed making sure he wouldn't pass out again. Molly, Ruth, and Luke all gathered in the wagon bed and got settled.

And before Molly knew it, they were off once again. Traveling through the hot sun, blistering air, and burning ground. Danny was soon asleep in one of the corners, which is what he needed, rest. Molly knew it was going to be a long ride as her forehead already began to sweat.

Molly looked off into the distance. The landscape was the same. Just looking at the sand made Molly sweat. Molly looked at Ruth and Luke. The poor kids were sunburned and very uncomfortable. They looked like little lobsters.

CHAPTER 38

The wagon moved ever so slowly, and Molly began to think. She imagined what would happen that night. She knew it was going to be interesting. Molly wondered about Klide Din, which Miguel yelled to Molly as they rode away. Molly wondered about her journey. Why was she going to Hawaii in the first place? She also thought about Ivan.

Molly spent a large amount of her time thinking about Ivan. She wondered if she could ever understand such an evil person. She knew she had to forgive Ivan at some point, but she didn't know how. The man killed her parents all because her parents knew something about him that he didn't want anyone knowing.

Molly looked around at the twins, who were drifting asleep in the hot sun. It was most likely around one in the afternoon. Danny was slowly waking up. He hadn't eaten anything since his little tumble earlier that morning.

Molly wondered if she should've even left the orphanage. She felt kind of bad as she thought of Danny and twins and Harvey Jones. She felt like she had dragged them into her little get away. Molly tried to think of what she would be doing right now if she had stayed at the orphanage and she knew exactly what she would be doing. She would be exploring the alley ways. The nooks and crannies of New York City.

Molly Grace thought highly of New York City for it had

been her home, where she grew up. However, just like any place, New York City had a somewhat dark side. Molly had seen both the beautiful things in New York City, but she also knew of the things that were not so good.

Even though Molly was only fourteen, she had run into quite a few bad people in her life, not to mention Ivan. Molly remembered she used to have a friend. His name was Bobby Chive. He owned a sandwich shop in the "not so good" part of town. Bobby was a large old man. He was quite tall and his big belly stuck out very far. Molly thought highly of Bobby; he was a kind old man who cared for many people, including her.

Molly was eleven at the time. She had gone to sleep and woken up just like usual. However, when she decided to go see Bobby Chive later that afternoon, the surprise she got was anything but good. During the night, poor old Bobby's store and restaurant had been robbed.

Molly remembered walking up to the scene. There were five police men, two of whom had notepads. There were a few police cars and one ambulance. There were a couple who stopped and looked at what was happening, but most people were oblivious to the tragic event that had taken place.

Molly walked up to the door of the shop. There was tape everywhere so she could not enter. There was glass on the ground from where the robber or robbers had shattered the windows. Molly looked inside and saw the deli counter had been broken and sandwiches were everywhere.

The tables and chairs had all been flipped over or broken and the charity jar Bobby always kept on the counter was also shattered on the ground, empty as can be. Molly turned around and saw into the ambulance. The doors were wide open and underneath a white sheet, two big feet hung out in brown shoes.

One of the nurses was talking to two police officers. The officers were nodding their heads and then the nurse walked off and closed the ambulance doors. Molly ran up to one of the officers and asked him what had happened. He told her the old man's store was robbed during the night. He also explained that the man was killed; he hadn't survived the fatal blow to his head and two gunshot wounds in his chest. Molly slowly sauntered home that day. However, she never let a tear fall.

Recalling that day made Molly shiver in the heat. Molly saw Luke and Ruth were both asleep. Danny however was awake.

"Danny," Molly said, "how long have you been up?"

"Not long," Danny replied. The two looked at the ground unsure of what to say or too tired to speak.

"Oh, by the way I found this at that mansion we went to and then ran away from a couple days ago," Danny told Molly as he reached in his bag. Danny dug around for a bit , eventually putting his head in his bag so as to find what he was looking for. Then he pulled out a book. It was Molly's journal.

Molly's mouth dropped in amazement.

"Danny, that's my journal," Molly said.

"I know," Danny smiled, "I mean I didn't read it or anything, but here you go," Danny handed it to Molly.

"Well, thank you. I ... I thought I had lost it," Molly smiled. Molly was glad but mostly shocked to find her journal back with her. Hope might have a place in her life after all. Molly opened it to find it was exactly the same as she left it. Only two pages were full of words that Molly wrote in it.

The reason that Molly's journal had meant so much to her was because it was given to her as a gift. Shelly Crane had given the journal to Molly almost a week ago when Molly first started her journey. Molly rarely got any gifts. She was an orphan therefore she had little, well no family.

However, even though Molly's life had not been the happiest, she made the best of it. Molly realized that giving gifts is so much more rewarding than any present that she could get.

Even though Molly hardly got anything in the way or presents, what few things she did have were cherished by her. Molly knew very well that things and objects can only make you so happy. It's a choice if you want to be happy or not.

Molly stared at the floorboards in the wagon bed. The twins were now wide awake because the wagon was going through a very rocky section on the little dirt path.

"Everybody still here?" Harvey Jones yelled back

"Yes," the kids replied back.

"Well, hold on, we got more bumps in the road coming," Harvey said as he slowed the wagon down a lot and took his time steering the horses on the rocks in the path.

"I've never been on a roller coaster before," Ruth began, "But I imagine it's something like this," she said as she jerked back and forth. A few moments later the path was clear once more and it was a smooth ride.

"I've been on a roller coaster before," Danny said. Everyone looked at Danny in disbelief, everyone except Harvey, he was driving.

"I bet you haven't," Ruth told Danny.

"Oh but I have," Danny smiled.

"Well go on then, tell us the story?" Molly said. Danny took a breath and sat up more.

"All right well, it was in the fall of 1937," Danny began, "A few of my friends and I decided to go to Brooklyn, New York. I mean none of us had anything better to do. We had heard about an Amusement Park, Coney Island was the name I believe. So we snuck on a bus and then onto a boat and well that's not important. We got into the park and went straight to the line of the ride."

"The line was real long, but we decided we had come all that way so we were gonna have to wait in the line. Well anyway, we got up there, and they strapped us into a seat with a buckle. Next thing we knew we were flying and spinning and tipping and going really fast!" Danny said moving his hands in any which direction and doing anything he could to add effect.

"Hey, quiet down back there and quit moving the wagon," Harvey said, glancing back. Ruth and Luke both snickered under their breath as Danny froze.

"Well, anyway," Danny spoke in a hushed whisper, "It was unlike anything you've ever seen or done. It was really great," he finished.

"Well, that's cool," Molly said and then silence filled the air as no one knew what to say.

"We jumped on a moving train before," Ruth exclaimed.

"Ruth, wh-" Luke began.

"It wasn't too long ago," Ruth ignored Luke, "We were running away from our orphanage, well more from Ivan, and they were chasing us so we had to think fast and Luke here," Ruth nudged Luke, "Knew exactly what to do. He led us straight to the railroad tracks where a train was just now leaving. We were able to climb on before it started going really fast," Ruth finished nodding her head, shining, proud of her story.

"What about you, Molly? What's your crazy story?" Luke asked her.

"Oh hmm," Molly laughed, "well I'm, I don't-"

"Of course you have a crazy story, everyone's got one," Ruth insistently interrupted.

"I well, I've got one, well more than one really, I just have to think of one," Molly said as her brain began racing to try and find a crazy story to tell everyone. Molly thought and thought recalling memories she had thought she'd forgotten. She gathered different memories from different places in record time.

"Ok, I got one," Molly said, sitting up straighter.

"Well, go on then, tell us," Ruth smiled.

"Well, it was back in New York City, when I was in the orphanage. This was two years ago I believe, when I was thirteen. I had been at the orphanage for sometime now and had gotten used to most of the streets and what not. Well, it was December and the New York Giants in the Super Bowl facing the Chicago Bears. My father was never a major fan of football, but I enjoyed it.

The game was on December 9, and lucky for me Miss D was not feeling well. I snuck out real early and was out all day. Now at the time, I didn't know that the game was on that day, but I quickly found out. Eventually I ended up at the Polo Grounds where people were already gathering. And then I kinda snuck inside and watched the whole game. It was incredible!" Molly finished feeling excited just thinking about it.

"Wait, you were at that game?" Danny asked.

"Yeah," Molly smiled and nodded her head.

"Wow, me and my buddies watched it on a tv on the street a couple blocks from the grounds. We could hear the crowds loud and clear." Danny said.

"Yeah we didn't watch it, or anything," Luke said, "We heard about it but never saw it,"

"Yeah, it was a fantastic game," Danny said.

"Outstanding!" Molly added.

The kids kept on talking for a while about their different adventures until eventually, they got hungry and took a break from talking to eat. Molly guessed it was probably around three-thirty in the afternoon. The sun was ever so hot burning everything it touched, especially Ruth and Luke.

Molly climbed up on the front bench where Harvey sat steering. She climbed over and sat down.

"Can I help you girl?" Harvey said without looking at her.

"My name is Molly and no. You just looked lonely," Molly replied.

"Well, I am not," Harvey said.

"When did you get so stern?" Molly asked. Harvey gave Molly a harsh glare.

"Ok then, let me rephrase that. Have you always been so tough?" Molly asked.

"No," Harvey said.

"No you haven't always been so tough?" Molly said.

"You talk a lot," Harvey said.

"Well you don't," Molly let out a snort. Havrey glared at her.

"Oh come on, what have you done? Who are you?" Molly asked.

"My name is Harvey Jones, and I transfer supplies for a living."

"Something tells me that's not all you do," Molly said. Harvey took a breath and rolled his eyes.

"I used to be a ranger in a small town. I grew up there," Harvey paused.

"Well, go on," Molly encouraged, nudging him.

"I had a family there. A wife and a son. We were happy," Harvey paused, "Until one day, Indians came through. They slaughtered everyone, everyone except me," Harvey finished and for once Molly thought she saw some sadness in the old man's eyes. Molly touched her hand to Harvey's arm.

"I'm sorry," Molly said.

Harvey took a big breath and shook his head.

"It's fine," he said skeptically.

A few minutes passed until Harvey Jones pulled on the reins stopping the horses and stopping the wagon.

"Quick break, then everyone come back to the wagon," Harvey said. The kids climbed out to stretch their legs. *It felt good to stand up, Molly thought.* Molly walked up to the horses, Apple Pie and Carmel. She began to stroke each of their manes. Danny walked up to Molly and stood beside her as he began to pet the horse also.

"So, any news of anything," Danny asked quietly.

"What do you mean?" Molly asked.

"About Ivan," Danny replied.

"Oh, well no, not really," Molly said, "Well, there is Klide Din. I have no idea what that is though."

"Or who," Danny added.

"Yeah, or who," Molly paused. "I think something's gonna happen at Polacca, Danny. Something bad," Molly said.

"Aw, well, come on now, you can't say things like that," Danny said as he continued to pet the horses.

"Why not? Bad luck seems to go with me wherever I go and for some reason, I think going to Polacca might not have been the best idea," Molly raised her voice.

"Come on, Molly, it's not that bad. We'll get there, we go to the train station and board the train and Harvey will be on his way. It'll be fine," Danny replied.

"Yeah but what if it's not, Danny?" Molly stopped petting the horse and looked him in the eye as her voice got quiet, "We're being followed, you know that. And it's not some nice people who are going to take us in and care for us, it's Ivan's men. If they catch us Danny, they're going to kill us. Don't you see. They will kill us. And think about the twins," Molly gestured to Ruth and Luke who were messing with some bug on the ground, "We can't let them get caught."

"Then we won't," Danny said, "Molly, I get you're being hunted, well all of us kind of are, but you have got to stop worrying. Everything will work out."

"I don't know Danny," Molly took a big breath, "I don't like this."

Molly and Danny's conversation abruptly finished. The gang of kids climbed back in the wagon and continued riding. Ultimately, the sun began to slowly fall, and before they knew it, it was dark.

CHAPTER 39

The drastic change in the temperature caught them all off guard. It was now freezing. Molly could see her breath and everyone else's. Harvey had said that he was going to drive all the way to Polacca. He had to get there before one in the morning so he could get his load.

As it got later and later, Molly's tiredness eased into her eyes. Soon her eyes were almost completely shut until she remembered tomorrow was November 18, her birthday. She was going to be fifteen years old. The thought woke her up as a little flicker of excitement filled her, but it quickly faded as she reminded herself that no one really cared. As quickly as Molly had woken up, she fell asleep even faster. With her arms wrapped around her knees, which were snuggled up under her neck, she dozed off.

"Wake up," Harvey's harsh voice interrupted Molly's peaceful slumber. She startled herself and jerked awake. In the distance she could see faint lights. They made it. They were almost to Polacca, Arizona.

Molly looked around to see everyone else gathering their things as their hands shook from the cold. Though the kids had few things to pack, it took quite some time to finish because everyone was fiercely shivering.

They slowly got closer as the few faint lights got a little brighter. It was not a big city but rather a little strip of buildings.

The wagon went right through the middle of the buildings. At the end, towards the left, Molly caught a glimpse of a train station. It was not busy though. Harvey pulled the wagon over beside the lumber building and got out.

"You four stay here and do not move," Harvey said sternly as he headed toward the lumber barn. He opened a big door and walked inside.

Molly looked around. It was almost like a ghost town. She saw a few people out on decks however they just stared with no emotion. Molly saw straight across the dirt road was the saloon. Normally saloons were bustling with people in and out, however, this saloon was not. Harvey Jones walked out of the lumber barn.

"There ain't nobody in there," Harvey said, "All right everybody out, we got to find where everyone went-" Havrey was cut off by a deep voice.

"Harvey Jones," the voice said. Harvey stopped dead in his tracks.

"I thought you were dead," the voice said once more.

"Well, sorry to disappoint you," Harvey replied back in a voice so deep and stern it gave Molly chills.

"No, it's fine, now I get to kill you twice," the voice warned. Suddenly a large man appeared out of the shadows from across the street. The man wore brown boots, brown pants, a black shirt, and a cowboy hat. His belt, wrapped around his waist, carried a gun and what looked like a couple knives. Molly shuddered at the thought of wondering why the man had so many weapons. The darkness kept Molly from seeing the man's face.

Harvey Jones stepped forward and began to walk into the middle of the street where he met the other man. They stood perfectly still in the middle of the street, six feet apart. Molly and Danny were on the ground however Ruth and Luke had not left the wagon.

Molly saw Harvey's hand slowly fall to his side as he moved his jacket out of the way to reveal a belt with a gun and knife also. And then, it was silent. Molly had never heard anything more silent. Harvey stood stone still, as did the other man.

"What happened to you Harvey?" the man asked, only moving his mouth.

"It's called age and don't worry, you'll get there Sam," Harvey replied.

"Maybe, maybe not. And it's Klide, not Sam," Klide replied.

Molly didn't say anything but nudged Danny, who nudged her back. It was Klide, Klide Din! The name that Miguel had yelled to her, it was a person!

Molly looked at Harvey and then Klide and she realized that they were going to shoot each other. Molly saw Harvey grip his gun tighter. Molly didn't know what to do.

'Wait stop!" The words left Molly's mouth faster than she wanted, and she ran up and stood between Klide and Harvey.

"Get out of here kid," Harvey said harshly.

"No," Molly said to Harvey and then turning to Klide, "You're Klide Din, correct," Molly could see his face much better now. He looked fairly old, however not as old as Harvey. He had brown eyes and big brown eyebrows. He had a mustache and a short beard, both had streaks of white and gray but were still mostly brown.

"What do you want, girl?" Klide asked, annoyed.

"Do you know a man named Miguel?" Molly asked. Klide Din's face relaxed and his expression changed.

"I don't know, has something happened to that man?" Klide replied.

"He sent me to you," Molly answered.

"What did he say," Klide asked. Molly had to think fast.

"He said you'd help us," Molly replied. Klide's eyes got real small as squinted so as to try to see if Molly was lying.

"He said you'd help us with someone," Molly said as her voice got quiet, but not a whisper.

"Who," Klide said sternly. Molly felt her stomach turn, but she said the name anyway.

"Ivan, Ivan Gualy," Molly said. Klide froze and then his expression changed.

"You keep quiet girl and don't you ever say that name around here ever again," Klide said in a quiet, stern yell.

"So you know him," Molly spoke quietly.

"Of course I know him, everyone in this town knows him," Klide said.

"Well, who is he?" Molly asked. Even though she knew quite well who Ivan was, she wanted to see what Klide thought.

"Follow me," Klide said. Klide then walked right past Harvey and towards the wagon. He walked around it and went into the lumber barn.

Molly stepped forward and began to follow him; however Harvey grabbed her arm.

"Don't you ever run between a standoff like that. I don't care what you were thinking, you could have been killed or many other people could have also. Use your brains kid" Harvey said. Molly gave a quick nod and then proceeded to follow Klide into the lumber barn with Harvey, Danny, and the twins at her heels.

Klide got a match and lit it, then continuing to light a lantern, he led the kids and Harvey to a door in the barn and he opened it, motioning everyone inside. Molly reluctantly went inside followed by everyone else. Klide looked around and then went inside and closed the door.

They were inside a tiny little room with a table in the middle and two chairs leaning against the walls. Molly looked down and noticed the dirt floor. Klide hung the lantern upon a notch hanging in the wall which made the room somewhat brighter. It was dusty and musty inside the little room.

Klide then continued to pace back and forth. Harvey pulled one of the chairs out and sat on it. The kids stayed smushed together in one of the corners and just watched as Klide paced back and forth. It was silent.

"Could you quit Klide," Harvey said, "You're making me dizzy," Klide stopped and looked at Harvey. He then looked at Molly.

"You should not have come here," Klide said quietly.

"Why not?" Molly asked as she stepped up.

"Because, this town ain't safe, not for you, not for nobody," Klide said.

"Why do you say that?" Molly asked calmly.

"Because," Klide paused, pursed his lips and began to breathe quite heavily, "He's here," Klide then sat down and put his head in his hands.

"Who's here," Molly asked.

"Him," Klide said with his voice shaking.

"You must be more specific," Molly said.

"It's him, he's here, in the town," Klide paused and the room was silent, "Ivan, Ivan Gualy is here, in our town," Klide said under his breath. Molly froze. Ivan was in the town.

"Where is he, Klide?" Molly asked sternly.

"At the saloon," Klide breathed, "he's got everybody. All the people, he's trapped them all in the saloon."

"Then why are you out here?" Molly asked.

"Because, I'm one of his men," Klide said as he put his head in his hands. Harvey tilted his head, then stood, and Molly tensed.

"Put both your hands on the table Klide, and don't move," Harvey said quietly but harshly. Klide slowly slid his shaking hands onto the table as Harvey motioned for Klide to sit in the chair.

"Klide, is this a trap?" Molly asked.

"No, but, he's holding the people hostage, my people, and I am supposed to turn in anyone I find to him," Klide said.

"Why is he doing that?" Molly asked.

"Because he's looking for someone," Klide replied.

"Who is he looking for, Klide?" Molly questioned.

"I don't know who it is, but it's someone who he knows," Klide replied. Molly paused.

"Klide, are they all in the saloon? Ivan, his men, and the people?" Molly asked.

"Yeah, he's got all of them," Klide replied.

"How many men does he have?" Molly asked.

"I don't know exactly how many, maybe ten or fifteen," Klide replied.

"And how many people are being held hostage," Molly requested.

"Everyone in the town, so that's maybe twenty or thirty people. Well, now there are a lot more people in the town than just twenty or thirty, but most people left when Ivan arrived yesterday. They took the train and left. However, the people that stayed got caught by Ivan," Klide shared.

"Klide," Molly looked into his eyes, "we need your help," Klide looked at the ground and slowly nodded.

"If Ivan is holding these townspeople hostage, we need to

rescue them, ok," Molly began, "We have to help them. You want to help them don't you?"

"Yeah," Klide said on the verge of tears.

"Ok then, we need a plan," Molly said.

Klide nodded.

"I agree," Danny said, stepping forward.

"I'll help you Molly," Ruth said.

"As will I," Luke added. Then, they all looked at Harvey.

"Well don't look at me, you know I'm with you." Harvey said. Molly let out a little laugh.

"All right, look, if Ivan has all the townspeople in the saloon and his men, we'll need to separate them," Molly said.

"What do you mean?" Danny asked.

"I mean, if we can somehow get Ivan and his men out of the saloon, we can get the people out the back door," Molly said looking up to see that no one was following her.

"Klide, tell me what the saloon looks like inside?" Molly asked.

"Well, when you first walk in, to your left there's a counter where the drinks are, some tables in the middle, a staircase on the far right wall that leads up to a hallway. In that hallway are four rooms, two rooms on each side, and at the end of the hallway is a window," Klide finished.

"Very good, now can you tell me about the back of the saloon?" Molly asked.

"Well, there is a back deck. If you walk in and go straight, passing the tables there's two doors that lead out onto a small deck. And if you look up you can see the window from the second story. That's really the only window though," Klide replied.

"I see," Molly said.

"I get what you were saying Molly," Luke joined in, "If we can get Ivan and his men out of the saloon, we can get the people out that back door or the window."

"Yeah, but we need a distraction to get Ivan and his men out, though I'm sure not all his men will come. Or maybe Ivan won't even come," Molly paused as she confused herself. "If we make a distraction outside, perhaps a gunshot or yelling or something, that would cause men to step outside and possibly Ivan, while that's happening, we would have to go around to the back and get in through that door," Molly continued.

"There will probably be someone guarding that back door," Danny put in.

"You're right," Molly sighed.

Molly and the others spent the next five minutes deciding a plan. They came up with many different ideas all while being quiet as mice. They had to think quickly and come up with a way to save the poor people being held hostage by Ivan.

They brainstormed and brainstormed, but eventually they had come up with their plan. And just like any plan, it had flaws, but Molly was determined for it to work.

CHAPTER 40

"All right, listen up," Molly demanded when everyone was done talking and they had decided their plan, "This is no game or play time. This is real, and if you get caught, you might die. Look, Ivan is no joke. He will kill you without hesitation. However, we're here to help the townspeople, we must save them and get them out of the saloon away from Ivan," Molly paused.

"If you don't want to go, then you need to speak up. It's ok if you don't want to go, and I wouldn't blame you, but if you do go, I need you. You can't freeze or get scared. We have to keep our heads, ok?" Molly said. It was silent as nobody spoke.

"We're with you, Molly!" Danny exclaimed, putting his hand on Molly's shoulder. Molly looked around to see Harvey ready as ever, Ruth and Luke both had their serious faces on, and Klide was nodding and reassuring himself. Molly looked at Danny who was smiling and she felt more at ease.

"Thank you all," Molly expressed. Everyone just nodded their heads.

"No, thank you," Klide said standing up, "Ivan is an evil man, and without you all, he might not ever leave. Truly, thank-" a harsh voice interrupted Klide.

"Klide!" The voice startled everyone and silence followed.

"Klide Din, where are you?" the voice got louder.

"I must go," Klide said.

"Remember the plan, Klide. Everything will be fine," Molly said. Klide nodded and opened the door and grabbed the lantern. He walked where the voices were calling him. Klide left the door cracked so no one could see the kids and Harvey inside the dark room and so they could get out easily to carry out the plan.

"Klide Din," a voice called. However this voice was different. It meant business. It was Ivan's voice. Molly tensed at hearing Ivan.

"I'm here, right here," they heard Klide say. The conversation between Klide and Ivan was muffled as Klide went into the saloon.

"Is it time?" Danny asked. Molly nodded.

"Yes. It is time," Molly said. She looked once at everyone's dark faces, she could only make out their figures, but she smiled anyway.

"Well, let's go then," Harvey said, going first out the door, "We'll be fine everyone, just remember to keep your heads. They're just a bunch of scared men taking orders from a bully, don't be frightened," Harvey finished walking slowly out of the small room into the dark barn.

No one was in the barn thankfully. Molly and Harvey walked slowly out followed by Danny and the twins. Harvey peeped his head out of the barn and across the road he could see the saloon.

He turned back around to face the kids.

"All right, there are four men outside on the deck. There must be most of them inside and two or three on the back door," Harvey paused and reached into his belt and grabbed a pistol, "Here," He tossed a pistol to Danny, "It might be small but it's mighty," Then Harvey gave another pistol to Molly. "You hold on to that and don't shoot me. You aim it at a bad guy and pull the trigger, but careful it might knock you over," Then Harvey pulled out another pistol and kept it in his hands. Molly wondered how many pistols he had.

Lets go," Harvey finished as he walked outside the barn and onto the road with Molly right by his side. Lucky for them, the four men on the deck were all busy in a chit-chat and Danny and the twins were able to go around to the side of the saloon. They stayed leaning against the wall on the side of the building out of sight from the four men, but in perfect view of Molly and Harvey. They were going to stay there until Molly and Harvey had started the distraction.

Harvey looked down at Molly and she looked up at him and nodded. Then Harvey tightened his grip on his pistol.

"If they began to shoot at us, you get out of here," Harvey said and before Molly could answer he started the plan.

"Hey fellows," Harvey yelled at the four men. The four men jerked and grabbed the pistols.

"Who are you?" one said, aiming a pistol at Harvey.

"State your business?" another said. The four men were obviously startled and quite nervous.

"Relax my friends, relax," Harvey said.

"My partner and I," Harvey gestured to Molly, "Have heard of a man that is supposed to be here. Ivan, I believe his name is. Well, anyway, we are the best gun men in the West," Harvey said.

"So?" one man said.

"So, let us meet your....Ivan and we'll let you live," Harvey finished with a smile. The men looked back and forth until one yelled inside.

Harvey stood still as a metal door and with as little emotion as rock. Molly just kept waiting for Ivan to walk out. Next thing she knew, Ivan walked out of the saloon with two men at his heel. He stood on the deck facing Harvey and Molly.

"And who might you be?" Ivan asked Harvey.

"My partner and I are the best gunmen in the western hemisphere," Harvey replied.

"Well, how can I help you?" Ivan looked at Harvey and then at Molly.

"Well,-" Harvey mumbled the rest so quietly that even Molly couldn't hear.

"Speak up old man," Ivan yelled.

"I said-" Once again Harvey mumbled the rest.

"Is this a joke to you?" Ivan began to walk down the steps, "Do you know who I am?" As Iavn walked down the steps onto the road, the men were all facing out and so Klide Din was able to close the saloon doors without anyone noticing. Molly saw and she cleared her throat. That was the signal for Danny and the twins to go to the back door.

Molly saw them walk slowly around the side of the building until they were out of sight. Molly waited for a sound. BOOM! BANG! BOOM! Three gunshots rang out into the dark of the night.

Harvey put his gun up and shot the three men on the left side of Ivan quicker than a cheetah. Luckily, the men were very slow and frightened and Molly kept her head so she was able to shoot the other three on the right side of Ivan. She pulled the trigger more than three times and the gun jerked, but thankfully she held onto it tightly. Molly could hear gunshots coming from inside of the saloon. It all happened so quickly.

Before Molly knew it, it was just Harvey, her, and Ivan out on the street. All the other men had been killed or badly wounded.

"Well, you really thought this through?" Ivan said with a hint of evil.

"No, not really," Harvey replied.

"And who might you be?" Ivan eyed Molly.

"You know who I am, you monster!" Molly yelled at him. Ivan's expression changed as if his confidence had been lost.

He let out a gasp and his eyes widened.

It was scary silent as they all stood still. Harvey had his gun pointed at Ivan's head and Molly held on to hers tightly. Molly heard noises from the saloon.

From the side of the saloon, many people ran out. The townspeople ran from the saloon and scattered around the town away from the fight.

"No, no, no!" Ivan screamed.

"You stay still buddy!" Harvey yelled at Ivan.

Molly saw the twins come running around the side of the building, then Klide Din, but where was Danny?

Klide Din and the twins froze to the right of Molly waiting for something to happen. However, before anything, Molly saw Danny walk around the side of the building. She breathed a sigh of relief. However, there was a man walking right behind Danny holding a gun to Danny's head. Molly immediately froze.

The man viciously grabbed Danny and held Danny by his neck with the gun on his head.

"Let Ivan go!" the man yelled to Harvey as the man tightened his grip on Danny.

"Let the boy go," Harvey said to Ivan, in a voice that was very serious. Ivan smiled, pointed to the man, and snapped his fingers. The man pushed Danny forward, but then aimed his gun again at Danny's head and his finger reached for the trigger.

BANG! There was a gunshot and the man fell dead. Molly quickly turned to see Harvey had shot the man, but Ivan had put a knife in Harvey's chest.

"No!" Molly screamed as Harvey fell hard on the ground. Molly aimed her gun at Ivan who was running towards the train station and she pulled the trigger waiting for the bang, but there was none. She was out, Molly had shot all her bullets and before she could even reload Ivan had hopped on a train and disappeared into the night.

Molly dropped the gun and fell to her knees. She just lost Ivan. Just like that. He was gone once more. Molly looked down at Harvey Jones who laid on his back staring at the stars.

"Harvey?" Molly whispered. Harvey moved his eyes and looked at Molly.

"Don't cry kid," Harvey said coughing a little, "You got a job to finish," Harvey insisted. Then Harvey Jones relaxed and laid his head as he looked at the stars. He took a big breath and let it out, however, he didn't breathe in again. Molly froze. Her hands began to shake just looking at Harvey. He was dead.

Danny walked slowly beside her and kneeled down. He closed Harvey's eyes and then sat with Molly just looking at the still body. The twins came and sat also. They sat there for what felt like forever.

"He was a good man," Klide Din said, walking around the kids to the other side of Harvey.

"Though we had our differences, he was a good man. A brave man," Klide said before a few moments passed.

"We should probably get him out of the road," Klide paused, "You kids need to go get some rest now. Go to Miss Kat's cafe'. She'll take care of you. Go on now," Klide finished. The twins stood up, then Danny. Molly knew that just sitting there was not going to do anything. She stood up with wobbling knees.

The kids then walked a couple buildings down and went inside Miss Kat's cafe'. Molly was somewhat in shock and everything was blurry to her. She felt sick to her stomach, for their guide and friend, Harvey Jones, was dead.

CHAPTER 41

Molly Grace stared at nothing with no expression. She felt no emotion, only confusion. She sat in a chair at Miss Kat's Cafe with a cup of water in her hands. Molly had lost track of time of how long she had sat in that chair. Not moving, not talking, hardly breathing, Molly stayed motionless for the longest time.

"Honey, it's almost morning, you need to eat something," Miss Kat, the owner of the cafe, came up and said to Molly. Molly just shook her head.

"Uh, no thank you," Molly replied and she entered back into her own world. Everytime Molly thought about what happened just a few hours ago, she felt sick and dizzy. Molly kept replaying the image of Harvey Jones' cold dead figure lying in the street. His empty eyes and motionless body. It took all her strength to keep from crying.

Molly didn't know what to think of Ivan. She didn't want to think of Ivan. The man had killed her parents and now he had murdered her friend. Molly blamed herself for Harvey's death. She knew Harvey didn't have to help her. But he did. Harvey Jones stayed with Molly in the fight and till the very end. He hardly knew her, but yet was willing to die standing beside her.

"Molly," the voice said.

"Molly!" There it was again. Molly looked up and saw that Danny had pulled up a chair from across her.

"Molly, how are you doing?" Danny asked as he sat down.

Molly just stared at Danny.

"I've been better," Molly replied, "How are you?"

"I'm ok," Danny paused, "I'm sorry Molly."

"Why?" Molly asked.

"It was me, Harvey chose to save me. If only I hadn't gotten caught, Harvey would still be here," Danny said, his eyes stuck on the ground.

"You don't know that, Danny," Molly replied.

"But you saw it, Harvey knew what he was doing when he chose to shoot the guy behind me. Harvey knew…" Danny ended. It was quiet for a moment.

"Danny, you can't blame yourself. If Harvey chose to save you, then you should thank him. Harvey was a brave man, and he thought highly of you. Don't spend the rest of your life mourning him, but remember him as the man he was. Brave and stubborn," Molly paused, realizing she wasn't just helping Danny, but helping herself also. She realized that what she just said was true and she needed to believe it. Molly and Danny sat still for another hour until the sun had fully risen.

"Where are the twins?" Molly asked.

"They're in a bedroom upstairs, asleep," Danny replied.

"Danny, we can't put them in danger," Molly said.

"What do you mean?" Danny asked.

"I mean, Harvey is dead because of my journey. I won't let the twins, or you, get killed because of me," Molly told him.

"Look, I'm with you Molly, all the way, but the twins chose to come with us, we can't change that. They know the risk, they know about Ivan. As soon as we can get them to Pasadena in California, we'll be good and headed to Hawaii," Danny finished.

"You make it sound so easy," Molly said.

"Well, I mean, it will be," Danny replied.

"You forget about Ivan, Danny," Molly paused, "Ivan is still out there, ready to kill us and anyone else," Danny took a breath in and nodded.

"Then, we just have to be ready," Danny hinted, glancing up at Molly. Molly looked at Danny's blue eyes and felt better than before. Molly and Danny then stood up to go out into the main room of the cafe where everyone was waiting. They began to walk, but Molly grabbed Danny's arm.

"Thank you Danny. I've never had a friend before, but you're pretty great. Thanks for sticking with me," Molly spouted. Danny showed a half smile and reassuring nod. Then the two walked into the main room where the twins were sitting at a table and Miss Kat stood in a corner talking with Klide Din.

Molly and Danny went and sat at the table with Ruth and Luke. The four stayed quiet as they ate toast and eggs. Klide and Miss Kat walked up to the table. Klide pulled up a chair, but Miss Kat just stayed standing.

"I'm so sorry kids, just let me know if you need anything," Miss Kat said as she walked away mumbling, "Poor kids,"

"What now?" Klide questioned..

"We're headed to California," Molly said.

"When will you leave?" Klide asked.

"Tomorrow, when the train gets back," Molly said. Klide just nodded his head.

"The town is doing a burial for Harvey later today, I think you all should come," Klide said. None of the kids said anything. Klide stood up and put his chair back, he then began to head out of the cafe, but he stopped at the door.

"You kids are something else," he stated and then walked out of the cafe, closing the door behind him.

"Luke and I are grateful to you guys for letting us tag along," Ruth remarked.

"It's no problem," Danny replied.

"We'll catch the eight-o-clock tomorrow morning and get to San Diego by seven at night. Then, we'll have to get you two," Molly pointed to the twins, "a train to Pasadena. Then, Danny and I will hop on a boat to Hawaii," Molly said. Everyone just nodded.

Molly sat at the table for a while. Not moving or speaking to anyone. She felt so confused and lonely. The twins soon got up and went to explore the town, but Danny sat with Molly for a while. However, soon Danny too, left to go explore the town.

Molly sat in the little booth for a couple hours. She had dazed in and out of the real world and everything just seemed like a blur. Every once in a while, Miss Kat would offer Molly something to eat, but Molly's appetite was long gone.

She knew that she had to get a grip and move on, but Molly just kept blaming herself for Harvey's death. The image of Harvey's still dead body and his eyes as they lost their life, kept replaying in her head and Molly recalled the feeling of defeat as she watched Ivan get away once more.

Molly had thought she had seen a sign of hope a couple of days ago, but she soon realized that she did not care for the taste of hope, for it was bitter to her. So far, Molly's life had been anything but like her dreams. She had lost practically everyone she cared about and there was nothing she could do to save them. Molly felt hopeless and lost and she didn't know what to do.

"Honey."

Molly thought she heard a voice.

"Honey, are you awake?" Miss Kat's voice invaded Molly's thinking.

"Yes, I'm awake," Molly responded looking at Miss Kat who sat down on the other side of the booth.

"How are you doing, dear?" Miss Kat asked. Molly didn't know what to say. So, Molly studied Miss Kat's soft green eyes and short dark hair that was pulled into a tight bun. Molly felt a sense of comfort around Miss Kat even though she only met her a couple of hours ago.

"I'm ok," Molly eventually said.

"There is no need for you to lie to me," Miss Kat told Molly.

"I, I" Molly took a breath and relaxed her shoulders, "I think it's my fault that Harvey is dead. And I just feel so hopeless and lost. My life is a mess, and everyone that I've cared about is dead,"

"You know, Molly, your life is not a mess. You have people who care about you. That young boy, he cares about you. Those twins, they look up to you. Harvey Jones thought you were one of the bravest kids on earth, and his death should not be one to cry about."

She paused, "Molly, if you really looked up to Harvey, then you would know that Harvey wouldn't cry about his own death and he would not want you to cry about his death either. He showed you how much your cause and your journey meant to him, so use his sacrifice as a way to keep you going. You're not finished yet, and that evil man is still out there. Finish what you started, Molly." Miss Kat patted Molly's arm and then she got up and walked away.

Molly was speechless. She knew Miss Kat was right, but Molly felt like all her strength was gone. Molly closed her eyes and squeezed her fists. Then she took a breath, stood up, and scooted out of the booth.

Molly advanced forward and opened the door of the cafe' and she stepped outside onto the dirt road. Molly looked to her right and saw the train station far down. The sun almost blinded her vision as she scanned around for Danny and the twins. It was around one in the afternoon and the town was quite busy.

As Molly walked down the road, a young boy came up and handed her a piece of paper. Molly took the paper and read what it said. It was an invitation to the funeral of Harvey Jones. Molly took a deep breath and continued to walk along the road.

Out of the corner of her eye, she saw Danny, the twins, and Klide walking along the other side of the road. Molly cut across the road and walked beside Luke.

"Hey Molly. We didn't want to bother you, but now you're out here. How are you?" Ruth asked.

"Um, I'm ok," Molly nodded her head, "how are you guys?"

"We're all right," Danny said, "Just trying to figure out what to do about Ivan," Molly took a deep breath and rolled her eyes.

"Do you know where that train that Ivan got on was headed, Klide?" Molly asked.

"I believe it was headed to Califona," Klide replied.

"Ok, so whenever we get to California sometime later tomorrow, we'll tell the police about him," Molly said.

They all continued to walk silently along the dirt road until they got back to the cafe'. Klide and the twins went inside. Molly and Danny stayed outside.

"Are you gonna come to Harvey's funeral?" Danny asked.

"I think I should," Molly said.

"I know you should," Danny told her.

"Then I guess I will," Molly thought quickly to change the subject, "So, tomorrow, we'll catch the eight-o-clock train and be headed to San Diego. We'll get there around seven. From there, we have to get the twins on a train to Pasadena," Molly said.

"Yup," Danny nodded his head, "however, for tonight we need to focus on Harvey and getting a lot of rest," Danny said. He then walked inside the cafe' and left Molly standing outside.

Molly took a deep breath and tried to calm herself. It seemed as though the world kept on moving and no one cared about the loss of dear Harvey Jones

CHAPTER 42

Eventually, Molly walked inside the cafe'. Soon everyone left the cafe' and headed over to the church for Harvey's funeral. As she approached the church, Molly felt like each step she took got heavier and heavier. Molly stepped inside and took a seat in a pew. Even though Molly had seen a lot of death in her life, she couldn't remember the last time she attended a funeral.

The preacher soon got up and spoke a few kind words and then everyone stood to sing a song. Molly tried singing, but it seemed that her voice had left her. Then they all sat back down, and the preacher once again talked. Molly heard the first few words the preacher spoke about sacrifice and bravery, but she soon couldn't listen anymore and she zoned out. Molly sat still during the whole service and tried to listen, but soon Molly gave up and she entered into her own world, one which was much better than the real world.

It felt as though as soon as Molly sat in the pew, she was leaving it when the service was over. It was the longest, but shortest service ever. Molly knew that no matter how many encouraging or kind words people would say, Molly would never be the same. Molly had lost a friend and she was in pain. And no matter how much experience she had with losing loved ones, it never seemed to get any easier when it came time to say a final goodbye and to let the person go.

The rest of the evening seemed fuzzy. Molly felt as though she was asleep the whole time during the little reception that

Miss Kat held at her cafe after the funeral for Harvey. Molly sat in a booth in the far corner staring out the window. When she first sat down the sun was high and bright in the sky, but now it slowly started to fall as darkness crept over the town.

Molly looked to her left and saw Miss Kat chatting with some ladies. Ruth sat eating some food whilst talking to Danny. Luke, of course, was reading a book that he had found. The mood in the cafe seemed calm and pleasant. Though people were sad about Harvey, they knew that he wouldn't want them to be sad.

Molly thought about Ivan. Though she didn't want to, she had to think about him. She had to figure out a way to get him in jail. Molly knew that for a while, it was just her anger and want for revenge that wished Ivan were in jail, but now it was so much more than that.

Yes, there was anger, but the man was dangerous. He had killed almost everyone Molly loved. He almost killed Danny. Not to mention, that Ivan had deceived the whole nation! He was a German spy. The man was betraying his own nation and he needed to be stopped.

CHAPTER 43

Molly Grace had felt defeated for the first time in a long time. Defeated. She had convinced herself it was over. The desire to get to Hawaii, the need for a home, and a safe place, all of it was for nothing, she convinced herself. She had put too many people in danger and she blamed herself. She was at a dead end. She didn't know what to do.

Molly lifted her head up and walked out the back door of the cafe. She walked into the cold of the night, but it didn't bother her. She walked down the few steps and onto the sandy dirt pathway.

Slowly a tear trickled down her cheek. Then another tear came. She didn't want to cry, but it felt as though the whole world was crashing down and she couldn't do anything to stop it. She picked up a rock and threw it hard at the dirt road. She picked up another rock and threw it even harder.

She fell to her knees, because she felt the weight of the world on her shoulders and it was too much. She sat on the little dirt pathway, alone in the dark, and cried softly trying to forget about all that had happened. All the things she couldn't stop. Her parents murder, Ivan, Harvey, her whole journey to get to Hawaii, it all felt meaningless.

"Molly," Molly looked up to see Danny, who with a soft expression on his face, walked down steps and stood beside her.

"What are you doing?" Danny asked as he held his hand

down to her.

"I don't know Danny, I can't do it anymore," Molly said. Danny knelt down and got eye level with Molly.

"You can't do it, but we can," Danny refuted, "Now take my hand and stand up Molly Grace. You've got a mission to finish and sitting here in the cold and the dark, isn't going to finish it," Danny sighed, "We're going to Hawaii Molly. We're gonna get the twins to Pasendena and we're gonna get Ivan,"

"You don't know that Danny," Molly said, shaking her head.

"Molly!" Danny yelled and threw his hands up, "Listen to yourself," Danny paused and came back to get eye level with Molly, "Look, the only reason I ever joined you," Danny swallowed, "was because of the fire I saw in you. You had a passion and sense of courage that I've never seen before. That I've never had, Molly. You gave me hope that I could change my life, turn my future around,"

Danny stood up, "I get that bad things happen, and believe me, you've had it rough, but you've got something most people don't, determination. If there's one thing I know about you Molly, is that you won't stop until you're finished, and you're not finished," Danny held down his hand, "So pick yourself up, and quit feeling sorry for things you can't control. Harvey died because he believed in you. The only way you're going to fix all of this, is if you believe in yourself also," Molly looked up at Danny.

Molly knew Danny was right. She reached for his hand and he helped her stand up.

"Ok," Molly nodded her head and dried her tears.

"I'll finish it," Molly said.

"Good. You're not alone, I gotcha," Danny smiled. Molly grinned back and they embraced in a hug.

"Now, come on, I'm getting hypothermia," Danny said as

he walked up the steps. He turned to look at Molly still standing there.

"I'm coming," Molly said. Danny nodded and walked back inside the cafe.

Molly looked up at the big moon. She blinked a few times. This was it. She had a plan, and a friend to help her. For once in her life, she wasn't afraid. Molly had made up her mind; she *was* going to finish this.

She walked back up the creaky wood steps and into the cafe. Immediately she was met with sounds and smells of warmth. She looked over at the twins, who were quite content. Danny who smiled at her. She smiled at the sounds of people talking and the hints of laughter. It gave her courage. She took a breath and walked into the room where everyone was.

The rest of the night, Molly sat and listened to people's conversations. Every now and then she would chime in, and once she even let out a laugh.

That night would go down in the memory hall of fame for Molly. It was the night she knew what she was going to do and she had confidence and faith that her plan would work.

Soon, it was late and the people began to leave the cafe one by one until it was just Miss Kat, the twins, Danny, Klide, and Molly left in the cafe.

"I will see you all before you leave on the train tomorrow," Klide said.

"Well, we appreciate that, thank you," Danny answered.

"And thank you," Molly said to Miss Kat.

"Of course, you kids will always be welcome at Polacca," Miss Kat smiled.

That remark made Molly smile, but she had no intentions of visiting Polacca, Arizona any time soon.

Klide said thank you to Miss Kat and left the cafe. Miss Kat locked the front door and closed the curtains on the windows.

"Now off to bed, it's late and you all have an early morning," Miss Kat said. Ruth and Luke both laid on a booth bench and were fast asleep. Molly laid on another booth bench with Danny on a different booth bench on the other side of the room. Danny was soon asleep as Molly was left wide awake in the darkness.

She took a deep breath and reassured herself. She often wished that time would stop and she could live another minute in a moment, but not in a long time had she wished for time to come to a halt. She was in a safe place, with good people, and she knew what was coming. Soon, her eyes got heavy and they closed.

CHAPTER 44

"The train just got here!" Ruth yelled. Molly jerked awake and sat up. It was light out and the town was awake and moving. Ruth was staring out the window when she turned to see Molly.

"Oh good morning, Molly, the train is here. It's 7 by the way," Ruth walked past Molly to a table where Luke, Danny, and Miss Kat sat eating breakfast.

Molly stood up and walked over to the table. Seeing the toast and jam, and eggs, and biscuits made Molly's mouth water. She looked at Luke, who had jam on his cheek. She let out a laugh.

"What?" Luke said with his mouth full.

"You've got jam on your face," Molly replied and sat down to eat. She ate her breakfast and soon they were all packing their things for the train.

Before she knew it, they were all outside at the train station waiting for the man to yell "all aboard".

"Be safe kids," Klide said.

"Thanks, we'll do our best," Molly replied.

"Here, some extra sandwiches," Miss Kat said and handed them to Ruth to put in her backpack.

"Thank you, Miss Kat," Danny said to her.

"Of course kid, now like Klide said, you all be safe," Miss

Kat said, hugging each of them.

"ALL ABOARD," the voice rang through the little train station. People began to board the train, not many though. The twins walked up the steep train steps and got to the train benches. They each sat in a two person row with Ruth by the window. Molly sat by the window in the row in front of them with Danny beside her.

They all looked out the windows and waved to Miss Kat and Klide who waved back. The train jerked and once again Molly and Danny, and the twins, were off, headed one step closer to Hawaii.

It was going to be a long train ride and about an hour in, Molly took out her journal, which Danny had given to her before they had reached Polacca. She took a pen that Miss Kat had given her and she flipped to a new, clean page in her journal. She then wrote the date on the top of the page. *November 19, 1941.* It had been nine days since Molly had begun her journey. It felt like forever ago since she walked out the front door of Miss D's orphanage in New York. New York! That's so far away. Molly leaned back in her seat and pondered on the thought of they were almost to California, one state away from Hawaii.

Molly watched out the window as the train moved through the desert. She often would look up at the sky and admire the bright blue color. There were not many clouds, which made the sky seem ever so big.

Ruth and Luke were quiet behind Molly and Danny. Luke was reading a book, of course. Ruth was looking out the window like Molly, but she was slowly falling asleep. The calming atmosphere on the train relaxed the group of friends.

This was one of the smallest trains Molly had been on and there were few passengers. There was a middle aged man reading a newspaper four rows behind Ruth and Luke. Two younger women who sat on the other side of the aisle were quietly talking. An old lady who sat drinking some tea on the other side of the aisle. And finally an older gentleman in the back of the train whose top hat covered his face signaling that he was asleep.

In front of Molly and Danny was another bench, and then there was the wall that showed the beginning of the train car.

Molly slowly began to fade out from the world. The click, click, click, from the clock on the wall created a steady beat for her thoughts. The tap, tap, tap from Danny tapping his fingers on the side of the bench, helped to give character to her thoughts. And finally, the steady breathing and beating of Molly's heart helped to tie together all of her thoughts.

She began to think about what would happen once they got to California in eight hours. The train that would be taking the twins to Pasdena won't leave until the next morning, so they would have to stay somewhere.

This thought made Molly grab her backpack and open it up. She began to look through all her things. Journal, sandwich, water container, socks, and finally, she found a little envelope.

She pulled it out of her bag and set down her backpack.

"What's that?" Danny asked.

"I don't know," Molly said, turning over the envelope to try to find a name. There was no name on the envelope, so she opened it carefully. Inside, there were two ten dollar bills.

Molly took a breath and wondered how she got a hold of these.

"Wow," Danny admitted quietly.

"You know, I bet it's from Miss Kat and Klide," Molly looked at Danny, "Who else would've known where my backpack was? It was at the cafe the whole time."

"Yeah probably," Danny replied, sitting up straighter.

"We can use it to buy a motel room when we get to California," Molly said and put the money back in the envelope and back in her bag.

"We can't stay in a motel room, Molly. We're on the run," Danny said lowering his voice.

"We'll be in California, that's practically a whole country away from New York. And besides, they probably stopped looking for us a few days ago," Molly replied.

"I'm not talking about the government, Molly. I'm talking about Ivan's men," Danny said seriously.

"Oh, yeah," Molly began to think, "I'm sure a little run down motel is somewhere they won't look for us."

"I'm sure that's the exact place they will look for us," Danny leaned back in the bench, "And besides, Ivan is in California, probably waiting for us."

"Yeah, he probably is waiting for us," Molly mumbled. Molly let out a sigh and leaned her elbow upon the window frame resting her chin in her hand.

"What are we gonna do, Danny?" Molly asked, looking out the window.

"I don't know," Danny said, "I guess we should try and stay alive."

"Yeah, I agree," Molly replied.

"I think that once we get on the boat and head toward Hawaii, we'll be good," Danny said, "Do you know which boat we're taking?"

"Yeah, we're gonna find a man named Mr. B. Red. He's supposed to take us to Hawaii on his boat," Molly answered, "Shelly Crane told me to find out when his boat boards and get there early. We'll tell him that we know Shelly and Tommy, from the Runaway Cabin,"

"Ok," Danny said, nodding his head, "We'll just have to figure out about Ivan."

"Yup," Molly said, still looking out the window. It was silent for a few moments.

"Molly," Danny said.

"What?" Molly asked, still looking out the window. Danny didn't say anything so Molly looked away from the window and looked at Danny raising her eyebrows.

"What?" Molly repeated.

"Why do you want to get to Hawaii so bad?" Danny asked. Molly took a deep breath and looked Danny in his blue eyes. She had yet to tell him why she chose to go to Hawaii. She figured, after all they'd been through and Danny showing his kindness time and time again, she could tell him.

"When I was in the orphanage in New York, I got a letter. I never got any letters so this was big. Well, I opened it and it was from my aunt. She says she's got a place for me in Hawaii. She's a nurse. She works at the Naval base, Pearl Harbor," Molly said.

"Why didn't you just stay in New York?" Danny asked.

"Because, it was the same old same old. I'm too old to get adopted, Danny, and would've become a seamstress, or a waitress or something. I figured, I've got a chance to see the world and maybe have a home, why not take it?"

"Yeah," Danny said, looking at the ground.

"You're going to join the Navy, right?" Molly asked, making conversation.

"Yeah. I'm going to Pearl Harbor too," Danny said with a laugh, "Maybe we'll stay in touch once we get there," Danny looked at her.

"I'd like that, Danny," Molly beamed. For a moment, Molly was happy. She felt as though she had a plan, and a friend.

CHAPTER 45

Lunch was soon served, little finger sandwiches. The kids ate until they felt stuffed. Soon, both Ruth and Luke were asleep, with Danny not far behind them. Molly looked out the window once again and closed her eyes and rested her head on the window. The sun was shining right on her face and it warmed her whole body. She soon allowed herself to fall asleep.

Molly woke up with a smile on her face. However, the sun was no longer shining on her face. She looked behind her at Ruth and Luke who were still asleep. To her left however, Danny wasn't there.

She looked around the train, but did not see Danny. Nor did she see the older gentleman in the back of the train who was asleep not too long ago. The middle aged man was asleep, the old lady was reading a newspaper, and the two ladies were still talking.

Molly figured that Danny would have had to go to the back of the seating part of the train car, to where there was a door that led to another room of a few seats. In that room was another door that led simply to the restroom, but that was it.

So, Molly assumed Danny was in the restroom. Molly leaned back in her seat. Then she heard a door close behind her. She looked behind her and saw the older gentleman sit down in his seat. Molly caught the man's eye and he glared at her.

She turned back around and her heartbeat began to speed

up. Something wasn't right. She made up her mind to wait a few minutes before going to the back of the train to the next room. She began to wonder if Danny was all right. What if something happened to him?

She couldn't wait any longer and so she stood up and began to walk down the aisle towards the back of the train car. When she came to the end and as she stood before the door, she looked to her left and saw the older man. He looked up at her and after a moment he smiled and tilted his hat.

Molly opened the door to the room and slowly closed it behind her. The room was small. It had three chairs on the right side and in the left corner, there was a room with a door, and Molly knew that was where the little bathroom was.

The room was dim, for the shades on the windows had been closed and the only light was from the edges of the shades on the windows. Danny, however, was not in the little room.

Molly walked up to the bathroom door. She knocked on the door.

"Danny?" Molly pressed, "Are you in there?" There was no response. Molly began to mess the doorknob trying to open the door. The doorknob was stuck. So, she yanked it to the left and it clicked. She pulled and the door opened.

There on the floor, between the funny looking toilet and little sink, lay Danny. His face had blood on it and he was bleeding from his head.

"Danny!" Molly cried as she bent down and moved his hair from his face.

"Danny, wake up," Molly said, rolling him over on his back. Molly wanted to get him out of the crammed little bathroom so she carefully grabbed his arms and dragged Danny out in front of the chairs.

She opened a window allowing some light and she grabbed the hand towel and wet it with water. She kneeled down beside Danny and began to put pressure on his head wound.

"Danny, Danny, wake up," Molly said. His eyes fluttered and he breathed in.

"That's it, wake up," Molly said as Danny blinked his eyes, "What happened Danny? Who did this?"

"The man, the old man," Danny announced. Molly knew it.

"What happened?" Molly urged as Danny tried to sit up.

"I came back here to use the bathroom, and he followed me. He closed the door, and closed the shades, and then he told me not to mess with Ivan," Danny said as he took the rag from Molly and held it to his head.

"He's one of Ivan's men," Molly whispered to herself.

"Yeah," Danny said.

"Why did he beat you up?" Molly asked.

"I told him I didn't know what he was talking about, but he didn't like that. He grabbed me by my shirt collar and told me that Ivan would kill us if we ever tried to turn him in," Danny paused, "It's bad Molly. Ivan isn't playing games anymore."

"Well, why didn't the old man just kill you?" Molly said.

"I don't know, maybe Ivan wants us alive," Danny said. Molly thought for a moment and then remembered where she was.

"The twins," Molly said as she stood up and opened the door. The train car was quiet, the ladies were still talking, and people were still sleeping, including the twins, but the man was gone.

"He's gone," Molly said, turning to Danny.

"He's probably going to warn Ivan that we're coming," Danny said standing up.

"What should we do?" Molly asked.

"I'll guess we'll have to wait until we get to California," Danny replied. Molly sighed and closed the door to the sitting train car as she walked back over to Danny who was dabbing his bloody nose with the washcloth.

"It's time for this to be over," Danny said, walking into the little bathroom and turning on the sink to rinse the cloth.

"What?" Molly asked.

"All of this, Molly," Danny stepped out of the bathroom and closed the door, "We can't keep running and getting beat up," Danny sighed, "We've been dodging death the past few days, and I don't know how much longer we can."

"Danny," Molly let out a breath, "You've dodged death your whole life and you will continue dodging death. Everyone dodges death everyday, we've only been very close to it," Molly looked out the window, "but you're right, this has to end," Molly sighed.

Danny walked over to Molly and stood next to her. As Molly looked out the window, she felt a hand on her shoulder. She looked to her right to see Danny's hand on her shoulder. She looked up at him and he looked back at her. His eyes were extra blue because of the light from the window. He looked Molly in the eyes and gave a half smile.

"We'll be ok," Danny said. Molly blinked and then she smiled. It was just Molly and Danny. On a train. Embracing in the light from the window.

"Thank you, Danny," Molly pulled back and looked at his face, "for everything," Danny nodded.

Danny walked back into the little bathroom to look at his face in the mirror. His nose stopped bleeding but he had a slightly swollen bottom lip, and the end of his eyebrow was clearly bruised.

Molly opened the door and walked back into the quiet train car. She looked for the old man, but she knew he was gone and so were his things. Molly walked over to her bench to sit in front of the twins, who were both asleep.

Luke had his head tilted back leaning on the neck rest from the bench and Ruth had her elbow seated on the arm rest with her head in her hand. Molly smiled at them as she sat down.

She looked out the window as the scenery was still desert, but she felt as though she was seeing more green nature. Danny sat down next to Molly. He opened his backpack and took out a sandwich that was wrapped up in brown paper.

"You're hungry?" Molly asked shockingly.

"Um, yeah," Danny said as he took a bite of the sandwich. Molly let out a laugh and she turned back to the window.

Hours slowly passed by, but the scenery changed very little. Soon it was 5:30 Dinner however, was not being served. Apparently there was no dinner provided. They were half an hour from San Diego, California. Molly, Danny, and the twins talked and they even laughed a little.

Finally, it was six-o-clock and before Molly knew it, the conductor's voice was heard throughout the train.

"We are now entering the Santa Fe Depot Train Station in San Diego, California. We hope your trip was smooth and comfortable. Don't forget to take your belongings with you. Have a nice day."

People stood up on the train and began to walk down the aisle towards the front of the train car where the door was opened. Molly and Danny, however, stayed sitting in their seats. They were looking out the window at the busy train station.

Molly heard whistles, talking, brief shouting, and she saw people walking, running, jumping, skipping. It was the most people in one spot that Molly had seen in a while. Her heart began to race because she wondered how many of those people could be Ivan's men, or Ivan.

CHAPTER 46

"C'mon guys, we got to get off," Ruth said as Luke and her stood in the aisle looking back at Molly and Danny. Danny looked at Molly, who looked back at him and nodded her head.

Danny swallowed his worry and stood up. He grabbed his backpack as Molly stood and grabbed her backpack. They began to walk down the aisle towards the front of the train following Ruth and Luke. Ruth and Luke came to the opening from the train and stepped down the steps onto the platform.

Danny stepped down the steps, onto the platform, and he took a deep breath. Molly stepped down the steps and onto the platform. She was in California. So close to Hawaii. Through the weird and strange smells, Molly kept getting a hint of what she knew was the smell of the Pacific Ocean. It was salty and fishy, but it made Molly smile and almost cry. It was the smell of freedom and hope for her.

Ruth and Luke continued walking through the train station. Danny turned to see Molly standing on the platform right off the train.

"Oy, come on, let's go," Danny yelled toward Molly, pointing his head towards the twins. Molly looked at Danny and walked up to him. The two began to walk not far behind Ruth and Luke.

Molly's eyes darted to the left and back to the right as she frantically looked around for Ivan or his men.

"Molly, relax," Danny said, still looking forward.

"What?" Molly asked, turning to him as they kept walking.

"You look very nervous right now, almost guilty. Just stay calm and act normal, everything's fine," Danny said smiling as they coincidently walked past two cops.

Soon, they walked out of the big train station into the city. There were buses and cars honking as they drove down the street. There were posters of Uncle Sam on almost every window and building .

The gang of four stopped and looked around, unsure of where to go.

"We need to find a place to stay, it'll be dark soon," Molly said.

"Yeah, and maybe a place to eat," Danny put in.

"I'm with Danny," Ruth replied, "Let's get something to eat," Ruth said looking back and forth from Danny to Molly.

"Okay," Molly said. They began to walk down the sidewalk. The smells and busy atmosphere made Molly nervous. It had been a while since she had been in a big bustling city. Of course, San Diego wasn't even that big, just bigger than Taos or Polacca.

Ruth was only looking for a place to eat, and it was obvious. Her head spun to the left and then the right and then all the way around looking for food. Luke was looking all around as well. The cars, buses, newspapers, and people seemed to excite him. Danny had a blank expression on his face. He walked with both of his hands on the straps of his backpack as if he were afraid someone would grab it right off his back. The kids had been walking for a while. At least a mile, they had walked.

"Hey look, a restaurant," Ruth pointed and exclaimed happily as she began to walk to the left of the sidewalk where the entrance was.

"Hold up," Danny said, grabbing the back of her backpack

stopping her from walking any further, "That's a bar, Ruth," Danny said pointing to the sign that read, Tavoli Bar.

"Oh, well, so what?" Ruth asked, turning to face Danny, Molly, and Luke.

"So, it sounds like there's a bunch of angry men in there," Luke said. The kids listened and could hear the sounds of yelling over the loud piano music.

"Moving on," Molly sighed. They began to walk some more and saw across the street, which wasn't as busy anymore.

"Look there, Shadean's Diner and Boarding," Danny said, "Come on, I'd say it's our best bet," Danny said as he began to walk across the street. Ruth and Luke followed with Molly bringing up the rear. She jogged up to walk beside Danny.

"I thought you said we shouldn't stay in a hotel," Molly said quietly, but forcefully.

"This is a boarding place," Danny clarified as they walked up on the other side of the street onto the sidewalk.

"It's a hotel, Danny," Molly said as she stopped walking. Danny turned to face her.

"What is going on?" Luke asked and the four all stopped walking to the side of the not busy sidewalk. Danny looked at Molly. Molly rolled her eyes and sighed.

"Danny was beaten up on the train by one of Ivan's men," Molly said.

"Well, we figured that out," Ruth snorted, "He looks like he was in a bar fight."

"Why didn't you tell us?" Luke asked.

"Because we didn't want to worry you," Danny put in.

"You guys are almost to Pasadena and once you get to the Runaway Cabin, you'll be safe, and you won't have to worry about Ivan again," Molly said.

"We know that," Luke said as he lowered his voice, "But we're not at the Runaway Cabin, and we're not safe yet," Luke paused, " Ivan is in California, we all know that," he finished.

Nobody said anything. The thought made Molly shiver only because she knew he was right.

"So what are we going to do," Ruth asked.

"We're going to stay here for the night and enjoy a meal. And in the morning you two will get your train to Pasadena and Molly and I will get a boat to Hawaii," Danny said.

"What about Ivan?" Molly asked. Again, it was quiet.

"We have to tell someone," Ruth pushed.

"Who?" Danny replied with his voice getting louder, "Who can we trust?"

"We can inform the police," Ruth mentioned.

"You really think they'll believe a bunch of runaway kids when we tell them that a German spy is in America with his underground network," Danny replied leaving them all speechless.

"Danny, we have to try," Molly announced looking at him.

"You're right," Danny stepped closer and lowered his voice, "we have to try to stay alive."

CHAPTER 47

It was quiet for a moment as they all gathered their thoughts.

"Fine, Danny," Molly said, "We'll stay here for the night," Danny nodded his head.

Ruth looked at Molly unsure as Danny began to walk to the front door of Shadean's Diner and Boarding. Reluctantly, the twins and Molly followed Danny.

The sun was beginning to set as the four kids walked up the four steps to the two front doors. Danny opened the door, and they all walked inside. It was a little musty inside, but the sound of the piano welcomed the gang.

To the left was a front desk with a man reading a newspaper. He had on a black suit, a black top hat, a monocle, and what looked like the beginnings of a beard. In the middle of the room, there were stairs that went up, and to the right there was one sofa, two chairs beside a little table, and a piano.

The man playing the piano had on dirty pants, a plain white shirt, and a newsboy's hat. He played the piano so softly and skillfully.

"Howdy, how can I help you?" the man behind the desk said. Danny stepped forward.

"Hi, um, could we have a room?" Danny asked. The man began to flip through some books and then he looked up.

"Just one?" the man asked.

"Well, how much does it cost for one room?" Danny replied.

"Three dollars for one room. A bed, and the bathroom is at the end of the hall to the right at the top of the stairs, breakfast and dinner are provided," the man said.

"Ok, um," Danny turned around to look at the others. Molly and the twins all shrugged their shoulders.

"How about this?" the man began, "I'll give you two rooms for five dollars."

"Yes, yes sir, please that would be great, thank you," Danny replied to the man. Molly pulled one of the ten dollar bills and passed it to the man. He gave her five dollars in return.

The man wrote in a book and then handed Danny a key. Next, he glanced at Molly and extended his hand, which had the other key in it. Molly took the key and put it in her pocket.

"Up the stairs, to the left, all the way down the hall, and they are the two last rooms on the left," the man insisted.

"Thank you," the kids replied as they began up the stairs. Molly was in front and when she got to the top of the stairs, she turned to the left without looking and ran right into a man.

"Oh, my bad," Molly looked up to see a bushy beard that hid yellow stained teeth. He was a tall and large man who wore brown trousers, a blue shirt, and black suspenders. He just grunted and kept on walking. She looked to her right and at the end was a door that she suspected was the bathroom.

Molly continued walking to the left until she came to the end of the hall, which was rather short. At the end, there was a window. Molly walked down to the last door on the left and took the key out of her pocket.

"I'll stay with Molly," Ruth said. Danny opened the door to his and Luke's room.

"I guess, we'll say we can meet downstairs at 8:00 for dinner," Molly said.

"Sounds good," Danny replied as they both walked into their rooms.

The rooms were small but not disappointing. They each had one bed, a night stand, a small desk, and a mirror. As well as a bowl and a pitcher on the small desk. There was a small window and Molly could see the street when she looked through it.

"Well, this is nice," Ruth said, setting her back pack down.

"Yeah," Molly said, setting down her back pack and jumping on the bed, "One time, Danny and I found ourselves in a huge mansion, it was crazy," Molly insisted, sitting up on the bed.

"A mansion?" Ruth asked excitedly, "However, did you get inside a mansion?"

"It's a funny story actually," Molly replied as she sat criss-cross apple sauce and Ruth climbed on the bed.

"This man thought we were orphaned twins and took us to the mansion," Molly said.

"Twins? You two don't even look alike," Ruth claimed, almost yelling.

"I know," Molly replied laughing. Molly looked up at the clock, which read 7:45.

"We could probably go downstairs and look around," Molly said.

"Look around at what?" Ruth asked, "This place isn't exactly huge."

"Yeah, that's true," Molly replied standing up.

"You know what, I'm going to go to the bathroom. I'll be right back," Molly said as she opened the door and stepped into the hallway. She walked all the way down, past the stairs and knocked on the door. No one answered so she opened it.

She went inside and couldn't help but laugh. It was a regular toilet, not like the toilets from the train. She stood in front of the sink and looked into the mirror. There, looking back at Molly Grace, was a girl who looked tired, but happy. Even though she couldn't see it, there was determination in her brown eyes.

She moved some of her hair back. She had washed her hair in Polacca, so it wasn't that dirty. She grabbed a piece of twine that she kept tied around on her wrist and pulled her hair back. She left half of it down and tied the rest up.

When she felt ok with her hair, Molly walked back out in the hallway. She walked back to the room and knocked on the door.

"Hello," Ruth answered, opening the door.

"Are you ready? I'm going downstairs," Molly spoke to Ruth. Ruth smiled and closed the door behind her as they both walked to the staircase. They walked down the stairs and went to the two chairs beside the little table. The man in the news boy's hat was still playing the piano. Molly and Ruth sat down and Molly picked up a newspaper that was on the table.

The front picture was of the war. Molly's heart sank a little. There was a whole war happening. She was living through history. She didn't know much about what was happening though.

"You're really good at that," Ruth stated to the man. He stopped playing and turned to look at her.

"Thank you," the man said smiling, "Would you like to try?" Ruth stood up.

"Yes please," she expressed happily. The man stood up from the bench and Ruth sat down.

"I'm Ruth by the way," She said to the man.

"Robert," the man said, touching his chest. Ruth looked down at the keys and stuck out a pointing finger and pushed one down. There was a sound and then a giggle. Then Ruth pushed down, harder and faster.

"That's great," Ruth said laughing as she stood up. Danny and Luke came walking down the steps.

"Luke, you should've been here, I played the piano," Ruth exclaimed.

"Don't worry, I heard you," Luke replied, sarcastically.

"Dinner is now being served," the man behind the desk interrupted, "Follow me please,"

Robert, Molly, Danny, and the twins all followed the man to a door beside the desk that led into the kitchen. There were three tables with a cream colored table cloth.

The smell of chicken lingered in the air as the four sat down. Then a man came through a different door with plates of chicken, green beans, and rolls.

A plate was placed in front of Molly and her mouth began to water. Soon, everyone was served and they began to eat.

"This is fancy," Ruth said quietly with her mouth full.

"Well, we're fancy people," Danny replied, shoving a whole roll into his mouth.

Dinner went by quickly, but then there was dessert. A piece of chocolate cake. Molly's eyes got wide as she stared at the piece of heaven in front of her. Danny's eyes were even wider, for he had already eaten all that he could.

Time passed by as the four kids sat and laughed as they ate their food. Robert soon left to go to bed and eventually the man behind the desk left as well. It was just the four kids. Molly looked up at the clock which read nine-forty-five. It was late, but they were all very full of energy.

"Nah, that's when I looked at him and said, now that's just a taste of what you'll get if you mess with me!," Danny was saying, "And then I ran off, but as I was running," Danny was trying not to laugh, "I tripped and fell flat on my face."

"That's terrible," Luke said, laughing so hard he was rocking back and forth.

"I know," Danny said, laughing as well.

Ruth and Molly just laughed along with the boys. When they all caught their breath, it became quiet.

"Well, it's past my bedtime," Ruth mentioned, stretching.

"Same," Danny, Luke, and Molly replied. Danny wiped underneath his eyes from where he laughed so hard, he cried.

"Well," Luke let out a breath, "Come on, Ruth, let's hit the hay," Ruth nodded her head as she stood up and pushed in her chair.

"Well , l see you guys in the morning," Luke said standing up, "Erh, well I'll see you, Danny, in a minute,"

"Good night," Molly said as they both walked out of the dining room. Danny and Molly were left in the silence. They both sat across from each other staring at the table.

"That was funny," Molly said.

"Yeah," Danny replied, resting his cheek on his hand.

"I hope we can see them again," Molly said looking up at Danny.

"What do you mean?" Danny asked, looking at Molly.

"Ruth and Luke, they're going to Pasadena, and we're going to Hawaii," Molly replied.

"Yeah, I know," Danny looked back down.

"I hope we can see them again," Molly said looking down as well.

"Yeah, me too," Danny nodded his head.

"But, Molly, you know, when I get to Hawaii, I'm going to join the fleet," Danny paused, "I might not see you again," he looked up. Molly's heart sank and it was obvious.

"I'm sorry, but, I, this is why I'm going," Danny said softly. Molly looked up.

"I know, Danny," Molly smiled, "You're one of the bravest people I've ever met, and you just so happen to be a good friend, who's going in a different direction than I am,"

Danny smiled, "You too, Molly," The whole thing was bittersweet to Molly. She had known why Danny was going to Hawaii and where the twins were going, but now, she was close to them and she would have to say goodbye, again. It seemed that no matter how happy Molly got, it would always end in a goodbye. Molly let out a sigh thinking about it.

"I should probably go to bed," Danny broke the silence.

"Yeah, me too," Molly replied. Danny began to stand up, but the lights went out. It was completely dark in the room. The only light was from the window and that was the light from the moon.

"What just happened?" Danny asked.

"I don't know," Molly replied standing up, "Maybe they had to turn off the lights,"

"No, that's not it," a raspy voice said behind Molly. She turned around just in time to see a large man, but then it went black.

CHAPTER 48

"Molly, Molly," Molly heard her name. It was distant, but strong. *Where was it coming from?*

"Molly, Molly," There it was again.

"Molly, wake up," Molly's eyes flickered as she tried to wake up. She blinked her eyes and moved her head. It was a dark room. The face in front of her was familiar, even though she couldn't really see it.

"Molly, are you awake?" It was Danny.

"Yeah, yeah I," Molly paused trying to move her hand but realized it was tied behind her.

"What happened?" Molly whispered.

"They got us, Molly," Danny replied with his voice sounding empty.

"What?" Molly sat up straighter.

"Ivan, his men, they got us," Danny said.

"The dining room, the lights," Molly began.

"Yup, we should've been more aware," Danny paused, "You were right, we shouldn't have stayed in a hotel,"

"They would've found us anyway, Danny. You know that," Molly responded. It was quiet for a moment as Molly tried to look around. Danny seemed to be across from her. The room seemed small and damp with no windows. She thought she heard faint voices, but she couldn't make any words out. There was however, a steady beat above their heads. Molly soon realized that it was feet. People were walking above them.

"Where are we?" Molly asked.

"I don't know. I'd assume a basement with the walking above us," Danny answered.

"I don't even know if we're still in California, I don't know about the twins," Danny paused. "How could I have been so stupid," Danny almost yelled.

"Danny! Get it together. It wasn't you. We got too comfy even though we weren't safe yet," Molly told Danny.

"Are we ever gonna be safe, Molly?" Danny asked.

"Probably not," Molly let out a laugh, "but Danny, is anyone ever really safe?"

"They're gonna kill us you know," Danny replied.

"Way to lighten up the mood, Danny," Molly mumbled.

"I'm serious, Molly," Danny confidently raised his voice.

"I know!" Molly yelled back, "I know!"

"I'm so sorry," Danny whispered.

"Danny, I told you to quit feeling sorry," Molly emphasized.

"No, no, I am sorry Molly," Danny paused. "I should've listened to you. I should've been more mature. I shouldn't have been so confident in myself, I should've."

"You should've done a lot of things. I get it, but that was then and this is now," Molly interrupted him, "and we're not dead yet, Danny."

"You're right," Danny said.

"We can still make it out of here," Molly whispered.

"I don't know how you do it," Danny paused, "You've been

chased by a German spy all across America, knocked out, tied to a wall in a basement, and you're still determined," Molly didn't say anything.

"Hello," Danny said, "You're still here?"

"Yeah, I just," Molly looked up, "I'm the most scared person ever, Danny. My whole life I've ran. I ran from Ivan, from the orphanage, I'm a runaway," Molly let out a laugh. "But, I want to be done running."

"Me too," Danny sighed.

"Harvey Jones didn't run," Molly said.

"Yeah," Danny nodded, "luckily we're tied to a wall and can't run anymore," Danny snorted. Molly rolled her eyes. Then she heard footsteps coming closer.

Lights made a rectangular shape to the left of Molly in the wall. It was a door, and someone was right outside. The door squeaked as it was pushed open.

"Well, howdy," a voice came through. A big man in brown trousers and black suspenders walked in. Molly squinted her eyes because of the bright lights. She recognized the man. He was the man from the hotel, the man she ran into.

"Who are you?" Danny asked.

"Who am I?" The man got close to Danny's face, "I am your worst nightmare!"

"Yeah, I wouldn't argue with that," Danny said. The big man was obviously offended and even though he struggled, he violently kicked Danny in the side. Danny grunted in pain and rolled onto his side. He struggled to get a breath. The big man turned to look at Molly.

"And you," the man grunted, "he's looked for you forever. Boy, is he going to be happy when I tell him I have both of you." The man looked back and forth from Danny to Molly.

"Are you talking about Ivan?" Molly asked.

"Well, aren't you clever?" the man teased, "Do you want a lollipop?" The man chuckled, Molly however, did not find it funny.

"Listen, here's what's gonna happen," the man paused. "Just kidding, why would I tell you?" he said as he put his thumbs on his suspenders and laughed loudly as he walked out and closed the door. They heard his footsteps fade away as it sounded like he was going up stairs.

"Lovely fellow," Danny said sitting up.

"Are you okay?" Molly asked.

"Yeah," Danny replied.

"Well Big Joe might be lovely, but he's stupid," Molly said, "When he opened the door, I could see the steps that lead out. There's a table right outside and it's got a bunch of things on it, but I saw a letter. It was open with the envelope right beside it," Molly paused and lowered her voice, "It was from Ivan, talking about us. I couldn't read all of it, but he was basically saying where to bring us and stuff, but Danny, it was dated a week ago. That was right after we left the mansion when we saw Ivan."

"So, how did he know where we'd be?" Danny asked.

"Exactly, I think Ivan has more men than we thought," Molly paused, "we've been fooled Danny, we fell right into his trap."

"Yeah, but we'll make it out," Danny said.

"What about the twins?" Molly asked.

"Does Ivan know about the twins?" Danny replied.

"Well, he saw them at Polacca, and I mean the twins know him," Molly paused, "We can only hope they got away and are going to Pasadena."

"I also saw a clock, and it's like one in the morning, so it's still dark out," Molly remarked.

"Yeah I figured that," Danny said. Molly and Danny both sat silently in the dark of the damp basement.

It felt as though hours passed by. Molly fiddled with the ropes that tied her hands behind her back. However, they were tied too tight and too skillfully. She couldn't make them loose. Molly couldn't even tell if she was asleep because it was so dark. Molly could hear Danny's breathing slow down and she knew that he had fallen asleep.

Molly tried to stay positive, but knowing that Danny and she were tied up in a basement to be killed and she had no idea where the twins were, it made it difficult to stay determined. Molly wondered how they were going to get out of this. It would take a miracle.

Danny was right, they're supposed to get killed. Molly figured that Ivan would probably want to see them before they get murdered though. Molly wanted to see Ivan before she got murdered. She didn't even know what she'd say, she just wanted Ivan to look at her and see that he had failed. He forgot about Molly, and Molly was determined to end his evil schemes.

Molly fell asleep thinking about Ivan. She wasn't scared anymore though. Being kidnapped and kept in a basement didn't worry Molly. Perhaps it was because Danny was there. She knew that no matter what happened, Danny would stick with her.

CHAPTER 49

BANG! The door slammed open against the wall and Molly felt as though she jumped out of her skin. She blinked her eyes and saw Big Joe. He was putting a blind fold on Danny.

"Well, good morning princess," Big Joe said, "Meet my friend Robert."

Robert walked into the room. Molly opened her mouth. It was Robert, the piano player.

"You too, huh?" Molly asked. Robert shrugged his shoulders and knelt down in front of Molly as he tied a blindfold around head blocking her vision. He began to untie the ropes from the bolt in the wall.

"Now, listen closely, I'm taking you two to a place where there are a lot of people and if either of you tries to scream or run, I will kill the other. Don't play with me." Big Joe said. "No games and no one gets hurt," he finished.

"I'm betting that's a lie," Danny said. Molly heard fast movement and a body slamming into the wall.

"I am this close to killing you right now and just leaving you down here, you hear me," Big Joe said seriously.

"Yeah yeah, I hear you," Danny said, sounding like he was struggling for a breath.

"Good, let's go so we're not late," Big Joe declared. "We have a date with destiny."

Molly felt Robert's hand on her arm as he led her up the steps. Danny was right behind her with Big Joe. She could see light streaks from beneath her blindfold, it was day.

"Stay here," Robert said as Molly stood still. She didn't say anything, but she felt a person beside her and she figured it was Danny. She heard Big Joe and Robert talking quietly away from them. Molly tried to look under the edge of the blindfold, but it was too tight and too big.

"Come on," Robert walked over and grabbed Molly's arm. Then a door opened. She walked down a few steps and she knew they were now outside from the feeling of the sun on her arms. But where? She walked and then stopped feeling that Robert had stopped walking. He opened a car door and she did her best to get inside without hitting her head.

"Your turn, get in," Big Joe said to Danny. Molly heard a bang.

"Ow," Danny grunted. Big Joe chuckled and closed the door.

"You okay?" Molly asked.

"Yeah, I hit my head," Danny replied, and Molly snorted. They were both quite unsure of where Big Joe and Robert were. Then they heard two car doors open. The car shook as Robert and Big Joe got inside.

"Drive, Robert." The car started, and Robert drove. Molly couldn't remember the last time she was in a car. It was similar to a train, only with more turns. They drove for what felt like twenty minutes. As the car drove, Molly knew that her things in her backpack she had were gone forever. Including her journal, which was in her backpack.

The car stopped. Robert turned around and reached back taking off Molly's blindfold and then he took off Danny's. It was bright out and busy. There were people bustling in and out of the big train station.

"Listen, like I said, any tricks from you," Big Joe pointed to Danny. "And I'll kill your girlfriend here, and same with you," he asserted as he looked at Molly.

Robert got out and opened Molly's door. He helped her out and then untied the rope that still tied Molly's hands together. Big Joe and Danny walked around the car to Molly and Robert.

Molly rubbed her wrists with her hands. They were red and purple. She was surprised they hadn't started bleeding.

"Come on, and stay close," Big Joe began to move. Molly and Danny reluctantly followed as Robert brought up the rear. They all walked into the doors of the train station. Molly walked right past a police man and she tried to look as scared as possible without saying anything, but he only nodded his head and smiled.

Molly sighed. This was going to be harder than she thought. There were so many people, but they were all focused on themselves, and she knew that no one would even give a glance.

They walked past the ticket counters to the platforms. Trains were coming and going. Molly saw that the twins' train to Pasenda was arriving in fifteen minutes. However, Molly had no idea where the twins were.

They leaned up against a wall because Big Joe took up the whole bench beside them. Robert went over to Big Joe and whispered something, making Big Joe turn his head and look the other way. When he did that, Robert winked at Molly and Danny. Molly tilted her head and squinted her eyes.

Then, Molly felt a nudge on her elbow. She turned to her right to Danny.

"Look, Molly," Danny said looking to the left. Molly turned her head. She saw Ivan and two men walking straight toward them. Why wasn't she surprised? Big Joe stood up. Molly glared right at Ivan. He had on a gray suit and a gray hat. Ivan walked with a grin, but behind his temporary confidence, Molly saw something. He was scared.

CHAPTER 50

It felt like forever as Ivan took his time walking towards Big Joe, Robert, Danny, and Molly. Molly knew there was no hiding this time. No get away ride. No running. Ivan knew who she was, and she was right in his clutches.

"HAHA Ivan Gualy," Big Joe took a step forward as Ivan got to them. Big Joe gave Ivan a big hug, and they embraced like old friends. The two men just stayed behind Ivan with stern expressions.

"Jim," Ivan took a step back, "It's good to see you, and who's this?" Ivan asked, gesturing towards Robert, who was standing beside Danny.

"Ah, this is my nephew Robert," Jim said, kindly slapping Robert's back.

"Ivan," Ivan said, sticking out his hand for Robert to shake. Robert looked at Ivan's hand and shook it. Molly grunted and rolled her eyes.

"Huh, I almost forgot," Ivan said looking at Molly and Danny, "and how are we today?" Molly and Danny didn't say anything. Ivan nodded his head and bent down putting his hands on his knees to get eye level with Molly.

"Molly Grace, I thought I'd seen the last of you seven years ago," Ivan stood up, "Guess I was wrong,"

"Why'd you do it?" Molly asked with her voice sounding

empty.

"Hmm?" Ivan asked.

"You know what I'm talking about," Molly stood up straighter, "Why did you burn my parents alive in their own home?"

Molly felt a strong hand on her arm, yanking her towards Jim's face. Out of the corner of her eye, she saw Robert grab Danny's arm.

"Keep it down, girl," Jim spat in Molly's face. Molly squirmed.

"Let go of me you creep!" Molly yelled and yanked free.

"Enough!" Ivan stepped between Molly and Jim, "That's enough, both of you." Ivan grabbed Molly's arm, "Don't even think about running,"

"Why? You tired of chasing me?" Molly questioned, glaring at Ivan.

"Yes, yes I am," Ivan answered. "You're a stick in my plan, and I'm tired of you."

"Good," Molly said.

"Let's get out of here," Ivan said to Jim and Robert, "Remember the plan?"

"No, I don't," Robert said. Ivan sighed and leaned in towards Jim and Robert, while Molly and Danny were being held onto so they wouldn't run. Molly looked around the train station. It was still busy. People hauling bags. Heels hitting the ground. Whistles being blown. Molly tried to catch the eye of someone. Anyone. A train conductor. The policeman. The woman fixing her coat. However, no one cared to give a glance.

"Listen, we're going to take them out of here. I don't care where, an alleyway, a shed, but I'm going to kill them. And then we're getting out of here," Ivan said quietly.

"Why didn't we just kill them?" Robert asked.

"Because dimwit, I want to do it. They have followed me across the United States and know too much. It's time I get rid of them, and I don't trust anyone except me to do it," Ivan replied harshly.

"Selfish much?" Danny said. Ivan glared at Danny.

"I'm going to kill you first," Ivan hissed at Danny, but then a wicked smile spread across Ivan's face.

"I'll kill her first," Ivan grabbed Molly, "and I'll make you watch," Danny's expression changed.

"You don't scare me," Molly said looking at Ivan. "You haven't won anything. You're a sorry excuse for a human!" Ivan looked down at Molly and in his eyes, she saw pure evil.

"And you Molly Grace, are sorry good-for-nothing little orphan. You're a runaway with no family and no home. You're nothing and you will always be nothing," Ivan finished.

"They loved you," Molly replied. Ivan didn't say anything. "They trusted you," Molly continued.

"They were fools," Ivan said getting mad, "with a stupid little girl,"

"They considered you family."

"They made a mistake," Ivan replied.

"You betrayed them," Molly looked at Ivan. "You killed them."

"They were in my way, they should've known better," Ivan raised his voice.

"You took away my family," Molly raised her voice.

"You took everything from me!" Molly yelled, shaking her arm out of Ivan's grip.

"You need to hush," Ivan said, pointing his finger at Molly.

"Why? Cause you're sacred? Thought so," Molly was yelling at Ivan who was slowly backing up. Danny, Robert, Jim, and the two men were slowly backing up as well.

"You're a coward, Ivan Gualy," Molly shouted at him.

"You think I'm afraid of you!" Ivan stepped forward, "You think you scare me?"

"I think you're scared, cause I know your secret!" Molly didn't yell this time because most of the train station was quiet and watching.

"I don't know what you're talking about," Ivan said, looking calm.

"You're a traitor, Ivan. You betrayed my parents, me, and my country. You should be scared," Molly said with her chin high. Ivan swallowed. It was quiet.

"Ivan, let's go," Jim stepped in front of Ivan.

"Get out of my way," Ivan said to Jim in a voice that scared even Jim. Jim looked down and moved away from Ivan.

"I'm going to kill you," Ivan said so quietly that only Molly could hear.

"Do it," Molly challenged without flinching.

Ivan blinked once, and then with extreme speed and agility, he grabbed a gun out of his suit jacket and aimed it right at Molly. There were screams and people ran out of the train station. The one policeman, however, was nowhere to be seen. Danny dashed in front of Molly.

"Move Danny," Molly tried to move him away from Ivan's aim, but it was no use. Danny was selflessly willing to take the shot for her.

"No, now quit," Danny said. The train station became very empty very quickly.

"I didn't want it to end this way," Ivan bantered. BANG! A

gunshot rang through the air. Molly and Danny ducked and ran. BANG! BANG!

CHAPTER 51

More gunshots pierced the peaceful train station. Molly and Danny successfully got behind a train ticket booth. It wasn't only Ivan who was shooting though. Jim and the other two men were shooting at Molly and Danny as well. Robert, however, was nowhere to be seen.

"Come out Molly," Ivan bragged, "you have nowhere to go!"

Molly and Danny stayed quiet. They moved further away from Ivan, Jim, and the two other men towards restrooms that were to the side of the ticket booth.

"Listen, I don't want to kill you like this," Ivan said as his voice was getting closer, "Come out right now, and I won't shoot you. Maybe we could even work something out. I could be the family you never had," Ivan said. Molly looked at Danny and she gagged. Danny smirked, however, they had nowhere else to go. They could make a run for the restroom and potentially get shot or stay where they were and most definitely get shot. Ivan sighed. He had stopped walking.

"Look Molly, the cops are on their way. In a few minutes this place will be swarming with policemen who are gonna take you right back to the orphanage and I will just go to jail. So, no one wins. Come out and let's talk like adults," Ivan paused waiting for an answer. Danny shook his side to side at Molly.

"Fine, well, before you die, I want you to know that I did love your parents," Ivan paused, "They were my friends," Molly began to listen closely as her heart beat sped up, "however, I had a job to do," Ivan said. Molly stood up. Danny grabbed her hand and stood up.

"What are you doing?" Danny mouthed. Molly just looked at Danny, then she gave him a smile. Molly walked around the ticket booth into the open. There in front of her, a few feet away, was Ivan. He gave a half grin as he pointed the black pistol at Molly. Jim and the two other men were to his left and right.

"I knew you'd come around," Ivan said, but he still didn't lower his gun.

"You never answered my question," Molly said, "Why did you kill them?"

"Oh, you poor thing, I told you. I had a job to do," Ivan replied.

"You said you loved them," Molly looked at Ivan.

"Well, love can hurt," Ivan declared. "It was a risky business, and they just knew too much," Ivan paused and stared at Molly. "I should've made sure you were in the house when I set it on fire,"

"Yeah, I agree," Molly offered back. At that moment, Molly looked into Ivan's eyes, and she saw victory. Ivan believed he had won.

"Tisk, tisk, tisk, you're one sad little girl." Ivan boasted.

"And you're a pathetic little man who thinks he has the whole world in his hands when really, he has a gun and the backup of an old farmer and two deaf men all aimed at one sad little girl. You disgust me, Ivan Gualy," Molly replied harshly. Danny walked out from the ticket booth.

"What are you doing?" Molly turned, "You're gonna get shot."

"We started this together, and I said we'd end it together," Danny replied.

"That's sweet," Ivan chuckled, enjoying the images of the soon-to-be dead Molly and Danny on the ground that played in his head.

"Um, sir, why are you taking so long to kill them, we gotta get out of here," Jim said to Ivan looking around. BANG! Ivan turned and shot Jim in the chest. Jim dropped his gun and had a blank look on his face. He fell to the ground dead. Ivan turned back towards Molly and Danny.

"Jim, Jim, I have waited for this moment for a while now, and I want to savor the looks on their faces before I kill them," Ivan cooed, moving out of the puddle of blood that Jim was laying in on the floor.

"You're messed up," Danny said, to Ivan, looking at Jim.

"I am not messed up," Ivan paused, "It's just business."

Then Ivan raised his gun at Molly. BANG! A shot rang through the air. But not from Ivan's gun. One of the men to Ivan's left fell down holding his shoulder. BANG! Shots were being fired left and right as men poured into the train station. Frantically, Ivan looked around, unsure of what was going on.

Molly and Danny thought quickly and got behind the ticket booth. Gunshots were being fired at Ivan. A train horn sounded that was louder than all the gunshots.

Policemen poured into the train station. Ivan's other man ran, but got shot down. Ivan had nowhere to go. Shots were still being fired.

"Stop, we need him alive!" one man yelled, and the policemen stopped firing. Molly and Danny stepped out from behind the ticket booth. Ivan looked at them and then took off running towards the train tracks.

Molly's adrenaline was pumping too quickly for her to look around. She began to run after Ivan. He was still on the platform with guns pointed at him.

"HANDS BEHIND YOUR HEAD!" men screamed at Ivan, but no one approached him. Molly was to the left of Ivan, and somehow Danny had gotten on the right side of Ivan, a few feet away.

"Drop the gun, Ivan," Molly yelled, "It's over." The wind began to pick up in the train station. It was silent for just a moment. Molly could almost hear Ivan's breathing. Molly's eyes glanced from Ivan to the train that was pulling into the train station rather fast. When she looked away however, Ivan fired a shot, but not at her, at Danny.

Danny fell down. Ivan turned to shoot Molly, but she pushed him right onto the tracks and had just enough time to see the defeat in his eyes before the oncoming train drove right over him.

Molly looked down. There was no more Ivan Gualy. He was gone. There were only the bloody remains of dispersed body parts of a man who once lived. Policemen quickly ran up. They grabbed Ivan's men, who were shot. Molly turned to her right and saw Danny being lifted up by two redheads. They turned so she could see their faces. It was the twins.

"Oh my goodness," Molly ran up to them and hugged them all at once.

"Are you all right, Danny?" Molly inquired, looking at him up and down trying to find a source of blood.

"Yeah, I'm fine. He missed," Danny replied, shrugging his shoulders.

"You guys, I thought," Molly began but couldn't think of the words.

"We saw you and Danny get kidnapped. Robert came to us and told us what to do. He's with the police. He's been following Ivan for months now. Finally, he had a lead. We worked all night and figured out what to do," Ruth said quickly.

"I'm just glad you both are alive," Luke chimed in. Molly

nodded. Robert walked up to them.

"I'm so sorry about all of that," Robert said to Molly and Danny.

"No, no, thank you," Molly replied.

"That was probably the bravest thing I've ever seen," Robert looked at Molly and then at Danny.

"Robert," a voice yelled Robert's name. He smiled and nodded his head and then walked away.

"That's your train, you know," Molly looked at Ruth.

"Yeah, we know," Ruth replied, "It is delayed though." Molly and Danny looked at each other.

"We have to get out of here before the police come to us," Molly said to Ruth and Luke.

"We figured that would happen," Luke replied, "So we made sure to bring you both your backpacks," Molly was wrong when she had convinced herself that her backpack was gone. Her things were still there, in her hands.

"We put some snacks in there too," Ruth smiled.

"What's gonna happen to you guys?" Danny asked them.

"Robert got us a train to Pasadena. He's gonna ride with us until we get to the Runaway Cabin," Ruth told them. Molly nodded her head.

"And you guys are going to Hawaii," Luke put in.

"Yeah, yeah, we got to go," Molly replied. Ruth nodded and she let a tear fall.

"I guess this is goodbye," Ruth added.

"Yeah, this is goodbye," Molly shed a tear, "and thank you," Molly said as she hugged Ruth.

"No, thank you," Ruth said, looking at Molly, and hugging her once more. Molly hugged Luke as Danny hugged Ruth.

"Thank you both," Danny said, "We'll have to meet up sometime whenever you come to Hawaii," Danny smiled.

"We'll do," Luke replied. Molly didn't want to leave. Everything was telling her to stay, but she knew she couldn't. Ivan was right about one thing, she would get sent right back to where she started.

"Come on, Molly," Danny looked at her, "Let's go!" Molly smiled one last time at Ruth and Luke. Danny began to walk, and Molly reluctantly followed. They immediately put their heads down. Molly glanced back and saw the redhead twins, picturing them in her mind. Sunburned and a little dirty, but she grinned as she kept on moving.

They made it out of the train station and into the bright sun. Somehow, they made it through the crowds of people and police, unnoticed. They walked for a few miles, and the salty smell of the ocean only got stronger.

CHAPTER 52

It was mid-afternoon, and San Diego was busy. People were laughing and chatting as they walked the sidewalks. Molly and Danny, however, were not.

Molly walked with her head down as they stepped onto a wooden sidewalk. Thus, she ran to the railing. With her head down, she took note of the sand. She peered up. There it was. The Pacific Ocean. It was a sea of endless blue freedom.

"We did it Danny!" Molly exclaimed dramatically, taking in the blue water, the seagulls that flew around squealing at people, and the wind. The wind was so strong it felt as though it would just pick her up and take her away. Molly wouldn't have minded it either.

"Yeah," Danny nodded, "not quite though, we're not in Hawaii,"

They asked around for a man named Mr. B. Red, the man that was going to take them to Hawaii.

"Do you know where Mr. B. Red's boat dock is?" Danny asked one man.

"Oh yeah, sure, about a quarter mile that way," the man pointed right past Molly. Down the street, but it was still beside the beach.

"Thank you," Molly and Danny replied. They walked briskly. It was the longest walk of Molly's life. They kept their heads up this time looking from shop to shop and boat dock to boat dock. And then, Molly spotted it.

A red sign with yellow writing, *Mr. B. Red's Boat Dock*. And underneath those words it read, *Come across the ocean on a voyage of a lifetime*. Molly stopped walking and smiled. Danny stopped and then saw the sign.

They walked inside as the bell above the door rang. A man at the counter turned around. He had on a straw hat and a tropical button down shirt. His mouth, which was stuffed with a fat cigar, was surrounded by scruffy unshaven skin.

"How can I help you?" he asked with raised eyebrows.

"We're looking for a man named Mr. B. Red, could you help us?" Danny asked.

"Well, I sure could, that's me," Mr. B. Red smiled.

"Oh Mr. B. Red. we're so happy to see you," Molly smiled excitedly.

"Do I know you?" Mr. B. Red asked, leaning closer.

"Well no, but Shelly Crane sent us. She said you'd take us to Hawaii," Molly replied.

"Ah, Shelly," Mr. B. Red laughed, "sure, anything for Shelly. I'm actually headed off to Hawaii tomorrow. You two are lucky. I just have two conditions," he paused.

"Yes sir, anything," Danny replied.

"You gotta help me out on the boat for your pay. I'll teach you what to do and call me Mr. B.," he finished.

"Thank you, Mr. B.," Molly replied smiling.

"You two can stay in the bunkhouse. It's out back," Mr. B. tilted his head, nodding toward the door.

"Thank you again," Molly and Danny said as they walked out the door and onto a little porch. To the right was the dock that led out to the boat and to the left was a little shed. Danny opened the door, and it sure enough was a bunk house. It had four bunks, two on each side and two windows.

"Well, I guess this is home for the night," Danny beamed as they walked inside. Molly took a top bunk, and Danny grabbed the other top bunk. Molly layed on her back staring at the cobweb infested ceiling. Time went by quickly.

She had killed a man. She was a murder. She didn't know whether to cry because she killed a man or the fact that she didn't feel bad about it. She thought about Ruth and Luke. They were probably laughing and gabbing up a storm. Luke may have been reading a book while Ruth was probably eating a delicious dinner.

Molly, engulfed in her thoughts, eventually fell asleep. With a knock on the door, the morning came quickly.

CHAPTER 53

"Let's go kids, times a wastin'!" Mr. B. shouted. Danny and Molly jumped up. They opened the door and the sun shone brightly inside. They grabbed their backpacks and walked onto the deck. There were three people down by Mr. B. 's boat which had the name Ms. Trudy plastered in red paint on the side.

"Ah, all right, I'm taking three other people on board Ms. Trudy. She's a beauty, ain't she?" Mr. B. paused looking at the boat, "It's a small load. That man," Mr. B. pointed at a tall man, "he looks stern and tough, so don't talk to him. That lady," he pointed to a lady with brown hair and plaid pants, "she looks fun, and that man," he pointed to a rough looking man with a beard and patched clothes, "I wouldn't talk to him, so, mind your manners and lets cross the ocean!" Mr. B. exclaimed as he began to walk down the dock to where the other people were waiting by the boat.

"I like his energy," Danny said. Molly laughed. They all boarded Ms. Trudy. It was not very spacious. Not the cleanest, but most definitely trustworthy. Molly and Danny went right to the front of the boat and looked out onto the water. Danny looked back at San Diego.

"Get a good look, Molly. It's the last time you'll see land for a few weeks," he said, trying to breathe it all in. Molly looked back, but she wasn't sad she was leaving. Then, an engine started. The boat had started and it began to move away from the dock.

"This is it, Danny," Molly paused looking at him, "We're on our way to Hawaii,"

"Yeah we are," Danny said smiling. Ms. Trudy cut through the waters as she slowly moved further and further away from the dock.

Molly and Danny looked behind them, the dock was still close, yet so far away. This was one of the hardest yet easiest goodbyes Molly had ever said. She watched San Diego fade away and the ocean get bigger. Time seemed to slow down as Molly got closer and closer to Hawaii.

"Oy, come 'ere," Mr. B. yelled at Molly and Danny from the pilot's house.

Molly and Danny walked over to Mr. B.

"Aight, you can put your stuff below deck, there's rooms and what not down there, just don't take the fancy rooms. There's two rooms at the back, you two can stay there. Once you do that, come back up here for your first sailing lesson." Then he turned and went back to the wheel.

Molly and Danny walked past the three people who boarded Ms. Trudy. They were already chatting. They went behind the pilot's house to a door that led down some steep steps. Then there were small white doors. They began to look around for the two doors at the back of the hallway.

They found them and went inside. Molly's room was small, musty, and humid, but it was comfortable because it was hers. Danny's room was the exact same. Molly set down her backpack on the slightly raised bed. It had a thin white blanket and pillow on it. There was a small desk and chair right beside the bed and then a dresser.

She walked out of the room and to her left was another door. To her right was Danny's room. She opened the door to her left and found a small toilet, sink and mirror. It was a little dirty inside the small bathroom, but she would make it work.

She walked out and met Danny in the hallway. They both went up the steep steps to the main deck. San Diego was almost out of sight now. Molly could see the faint reminiscences of colorful buildings. However, the more she squinted to see them, the farther away they got.

For a moment, Molly allowed herself to feel a little ounce of joy. She was almost to Hawaii. She couldn't believe that two weeks ago she was just in New York City. A little orphan, all alone in a big city.

"Aight' this is how you sail," Mr. B. began to tell Danny and Molly. Mr. B. spent a few hours explaining the different ropes, directions, winds, sails, and waters to the kids. Then he called everyone to the main deck. They were now in the middle of the blue sea.

"Now," Mr. B. began while Molly, Danny, and the three other passengers sat and listened, "this is going to be a smooth journey across the sea. Today is," Mr. B. looked down at his watch, "November 20, eh, 1941, and we will be arriving in Hawaii on," Mr. B. began to count with his fingers, "Roughly December 8. We should have smooth and calm seas ahead of us. My buddy Rick, you won't see much of him, but he cooks all the meals. So, uh, try to not get sick and don't go overboard," Mr. B. finished.

Molly couldn't help but smile at Mr. B. He had a strange way of assuring people, but it didn't bother Molly. She was overwhelmed and was in a little bit of shock hearing that would be arriving in Hawaii in close to three weeks. Molly looked over at Danny who was smiling from ear to ear. Danny began to nod his head.

"I can almost taste the palm trees," Danny whispered to Molly. Molly laughed only because she felt the same way.

The next few days consisted of the same routine. Wake up early, go to bed late, and in between that, work and eat. Molly began to love the sailing life. It was simple, but still had challenges. One of those being the sun. Since Molly and Danny were out on the deck most of the day, the sun beat down on them. Similar to the desert, Molly got sunburned again. Danny, however, only got darker. Molly had to wear a big sun hat to keep her face from being burnt off.

"You look like a mom on the beach," Danny said laughing at Molly's big sun hat one day.

"Oh stop being rude," Molly smirked back. The two were at the bow of the boat, the front of the boat, in the mid afternoon.

"It's true though," Danny laughed again.

"Well, I'm glad you find my pain amusing," Molly replied.

"Oh come on, I'm just teasing you," Danny snorted. Molly laughed a little knowing Danny was just playing. It was silent for a moment as they observed the deep blue water.

"I can't believe we've been on the ocean for three days, Danny," Molly stated.

"Yeah," Danny paused, "We're free!" He looked out with determination, hope, and a smile.

"Not an Ivan in sight!" Molly exclaimed excitedly.

"That's because you ran him over with a train." Danny replied back.

"Yeah," Molly got quiet again.

"Ah, are you feeling bad about that?" Danny asked, lowering his voice. Molly shrugged her shoulders.

"Not really, and that's what bothers me," Molly said. Danny took a deep breath.

"I think you did the right thing," he paused, "I know it's a little hard, but you'll get over it," he looked down. Molly blinked and looked at Danny.

"Who did you kill?" she asked quietly. Danny looked out at

the water, and then he swallowed.

"He was a robber, a good one. I should've walked away when I met him, but I was young and alone. I was twelve. I met him in an alleyway. I got caught stealing some things from a group of guys, and they dragged me into that alleyway. They were about to beat me up. When he walked up, he took me in. Fed me, clothed me, taught me things. I thought he was my friend."

Danny looked down, "He encouraged me to steal things. I became good at it too. That's how I became the Boy Thief. Well, one day, he had a big plan of robbing the local bank. I was going to be the distraction while he took the money. We went right before it closed, so the vault key was still there, but a lot of people weren't. He got the money, and we were about to leave when a lady stood up behind a desk. There were three workers there and one customer. She was a worker. He told her to get on the ground, but she refused, so he shot her dead. We ran out. I can still hear the screams. The sirens in the distance."

Danny took a breath and continued,, "A few days later, the story came out in the paper. She was a mom. A wife. She was a good woman, and I did nothing to help her. I made up my mind. That night, I took a pistol and shot him in the head. I can remember him looking at me and then looking at the gun. He didn't say anything. I pulled the trigger and ran away, far, and never looked back."

Molly was a little speechless.

"Oh, I, I didn't know," she shyly said.

"Yeah," Danny let out a laugh, "no one does."

It was quiet. Molly wondered how, after everything Danny had been through, he managed to be a decent person. He had a good heart; Molly knew that. And he was extremely brave. Molly took a deep breath and looked out at the blue sea. The sun was high in the sky and shining ever so brightly upon Ms. Trudy and the ocean. Molly wondered where exactly they were on the pacific ocean. She did know they were getting closer and closer to Hawaii.

The next two weeks consisted of the same routine. Molly got a little bored of it, but she encouraged herself to enjoy it while it lasted. Enjoy her time on the ocean and her time with Danny. Danny was going to join the Navy, so she didn't know how much of him she would see once they got to Hawaii.

The month of December rolled around quite quickly. Her whole time on Ms. Trudy seemed to fly by. Molly's favorite part of the day was watching the sunset. She felt as though the sun was so close that she could reach out and grab it.

Molly thought about the twins. They were in Pasadena by now. Probably fitting right in with the Runaway Cabin, their new family. Molly thought about Ivan's men. They were most definitely getting questioned, and hopefully, Ivan's evil network was being revealed. Molly wondered what her parents would think about her.

She hadn't seen them for over seven years, but she still pictured their faces clear as day in her mind. Molly took a deep breath. She didn't even notice the salty air now and the smell of fish didn't bother her, because it might have smelled a little bit like freedom.

CHAPTER 54

It was December 6, 1941. Molly and Danny were practically shaking with excitement. They were so close to Hawaii they could nearly taste the coconuts and smell the flowers. The past few weeks were simple and calming. The storms stayed away keeping the waters calm. Horrible situations were smoothed by the salty air. The sense of glossiness made their arrival time earlier than what was on schedule; sometime tomorrow.

Ms. Trudy seemed alive as well. The atmosphere on the boat was lively and joyous. Everyone was smiling and cheerful. Molly's sunburn was pretty much healed and Danny had turned a whole shade darker.

For once in Molly's life, she wasn't afraid to be happy. She smiled and wasn't afraid to show it. She didn't have to run anymore; she was almost home.

That evening, Molly and Danny sat at the bow, like they normally do, but it was different. There was a sense of accomplishment and an undeniable feeling of hope. The colorful sunset over the pacific ocean only encouraged Molly's certainty about the good days to come.

"Here's to new beginnings," Danny expressed as they toasted their water cups.

"And here's to the future," Molly put in. They drank a sip and watched the sun. As it set, it painted the ocean. It reminded her of a canvas wet with paint. When the paint was still so bright and lively.

Molly had hope that things were going to work out as Hawaii neared. She could see a new day in front of her and could feel the hope as it rushed through her veins, telling her to keep running towards freedom.

EPILOGUE
Late morning, Decmeber 7, 1941

"Wake up!" Molly jerked and sat up. She saw Danny's face, wet with sweat.

"What?" she asked.

"Come on, Molly," Danny said as he raced out of her room and up the steps onto the deck of Ms. Trudy. Molly jumped up out of her bed and ran up the steep steps. The sun had risen, and the ocean was still blue.

"What is going on?" Molly walked over to Mr. B. who stood on the bow looking out at the ocean. He turned to face her. His face was red and there was sadness in his eyes. Molly glanced back at Danny. She knew something was terribly wrong.

"Talk to me," she demanded. Danny opened his mouth, but nothing came out.

"Listen," Mr. B. faced Molly and Danny, "Pearl Harbor was attacked. Bombed," Mr. B. looked down. Molly's heart sank. She became covered in goosebumps. She looked at Danny. His face, which was so alive and hopeful last night, appeared crushed and distraught.

"It was the Japs. They came flyin' in', right over Pearl, about two hours ago," Mr. B. shook his head and rubbed his hand across his face as he walked to the pilot's house.

"How far away are we?" Molly asked.

"We should get there late night er' early tomorrow

mornin'," Mr. B. replied. He stopped walking with his back turned towards Molly and Danny.

"If you'll excuse me," Mr. B. walked off. Molly and Danny were quiet.

"It's bad, Molly," Danny broke the silence. "They radioed all boats close to Hawaii warning them. They told us to turn back, but we don't have enough fuel to go all the way back to California. I don't know how many are dead, but it's bad."

Molly didn't say anything. She was in shock. She couldn't imagine what had happened in Hawaii. What was going to happen. She put her hand over her mouth trying to keep from crying, however she was too busy trying to picture what had happened to cry.

Molly knew about the war. The war in Europe. As much as it bothered Molly to think it, the war had come to America. American soil. American men and women were dead. Possibly hundreds. She could only imagine what was about to come.

It was no longer happy on the boat. The hope and joy was stolen from each person on Ms. Trudy. Wiped from their hearts with the news of the violent and brutal attack. Molly was heartbroken over the thought of peaceful Hawaii being bombed. People running. Screaming. Getting blown up.

She just could not see how such a gruesome act could be done. Yet, it was done. Molly feared for the lives of Americans, but more than that, she feared for the men responsible for the heartless bombing of Pearl Harbor. Things were about change, and Molly was stuck, right in the middle.

ACKNOWLEDGEMENT

Photos courtesy of S.G. Conrad

Format Design courtesy of P.G. Conrad

ABOUT THE AUTHOR

L.f. Conrad

L.F. Conrad began writing when she was only three-years-old. Completely fascinated and relieved when she discovered she could put all of her ideas in one place, she began putting pen to paper. Writing quickly became one of her favorite ways to communicate as she brought to life the stories that began in her brilliant imagination. Along with novels, L.F enjoys writing poems and short stories. At one time in her life, she used to wonder if she would ever publish a book. It is times like that L.F. wants to remind all her readers, "If you never try, you won't fail; but you won't succeed."